Charles John S. G. C. Garvagh

The Pilgrim of Scandinavia

Charles John S. G. C. Garvagh

The Pilgrim of Scandinavia

ISBN/EAN: 9783337287757

Printed in Europe, USA, Canada, Australia, Japan

Cover: Foto ©Andreas Hilbeck / pixelio.de

More available books at **www.hansebooks.com**

THE

PILGRIM

OF

SCANDINAVIA.

THE

PILGRIM

OF

SCANDINAVIA.

By LORD GARVAGH,

B.A. CHRIST CHURCH, OXFORD,

AND

MEMBER OF THE ALPINE CLUB.

LONDON:

SAMPSON LOW, MARSTON, LOW, & SEARLE,

CROWN BUILDINGS, 188 FLEET STREET.

1875.

LONDON :

PRINTED BY WILLIAM CLOWES AND SONS,

STAMFORD STREET AND CHARING CROSS.

PREFACE.

THOSE who may be in want of information upon travelling or field sports, will find these pages of no use at all. I have hinted no directions for the benefit of future travellers, nor even touched upon the facilities for sport.

With regard to Norway, I have only given some particulars of a time passed in seclusion among the mountains, nominally in pursuit of reindeer. To look back upon that wild and fascinating life, in comparison with some time spent lately in the South of Europe, is to see the whole North surrounded with a halo, which only this change of resort would give it.

" Iceland now ranks among the constitutional entities of political Europe," and if what is here said may be sufficient to remove the veil which has made this appear to be a land of everlasting ice, it will not be said in vain.

Or if it be received as a testimony of gratitude to those whose courtesy and hospitality bade me such hearty welcome to the land, one part of the original design will have succeeded.

31 PORTMAN SQUARE.
March 1875.

LIST OF ILLUSTRATIONS.

THE

PILGRIM OF SCANDINAVIA.

CHAPTER I.

ICELAND.

" Far in the Northern land,
By the wild Baltic's strand,
I with my *childish hand*
Tamed the ger falcon."

O revive after considerable time the recollections of a foreign land, one has to be careful in developing with truthfulness that which is remembered only in outline and may soon fade altogether from the mind. For the particulars I have in writing are so short, the task is like having to supply material to fill out, as it were, a skeleton; or, saving whatever may be stated here is true, to put a dream on paper. The foreign country here spoken of, which comparatively so few travellers have visited as yet, has been accidentally called Iceland owing to the ice which an old sea-captain, a hardy Norseman, saw floating once upon the coast; but merely saw it in one quarter, and upon no other side. This country also has been variously called Isafold, Froni, Gardarsey, Ingolfsey, Kjartansey, Fjallkonanfrid (the Pretty Woman of the Mountains, i.e., to whom the mountains belong), and Thule, Ultima Thule, which last was the name given to Iceland in particular, and Thule to Norway, Shetland, Orkney and the Feroe Islands in former times.

The frontispiece represents this " Lady of the Mountains " with her brow encircled by a coronet of icicles, and surmounted by a crest of different volcanoes rising in the midst. On her shoulder is the Raven—mythical bird of history, typical of the country, emblematical of Memory and

Intelligence—whispering in Iceland's ear news from the other countries of the world. In her left hand is the scroll of genealogy, telling her descent; in her right, the ancient kind of sword, to signify the warlike character of the Icelandic people in past days. Overhead is a sea-mew, to indicate not only the surrounding sea, but war also, because her battles were in olden time always at sea. At her feet we have two rolls of parchment, with manuscript in Runic character, in which the Scandinavian lore that once made this people famous has been transmitted, and transported to us over the sea. A log of wood is also at her feet, in memory of that old custom whereby the emigrant from Norway used to claim the soil and build his house wherever it might come to land. Fastened on her bosom, like a brooch, is the celebrated star with five points that from time immemorial has been emblematical of wisdom, both in ancient Greece, and previously (as Urim on the breast-plate)

among the Hebrews.   I am indebted to a very
learned Icelander, Eiríkr Magnusson, for having
embodied these ideas, in a manner so expressive
of his country ; and for having presented me also
with a book upon its legends and traditions.

It was on board the Danish mail steamboat
(which had been formerly a man-of-war) that I
rose on a Wednesday morning of July 1872, and
saw in the far horizon a great stretch of snowclad
heights and snowy peaks, that stole upon the
senses like a vision.   Sharp and distinct upon the
northern sky, they might have been within easy
distance, so clear is the atmosphere of that Arctic
climate, so calm was the Atlantic on that day.
These mountains, all snow covered, were the
great Orœfa Yokul, Skeidara, Klofa and Skaptar
Yokul, stretching far inland, forming a region that
has never yet been thoroughly explored.   Etna is
higher than any mountain in Iceland, and said to
be 180 miles in circumference, but "if Skaptar
Yokul were hollowed out, both Etna and

Vesuvius might go inside and not fill it." And this volcano, Skaptar Yokul, once overwhelmed a vast extent of Iceland with destruction, desolating the whole country with lava, ashes, and suffocating smoke for many miles around, killing cattle, and driving many thousands of the inhabitants far away from house and home. Yet it has been said that Iceland and Greenland should change names, " for Iceland, notwithstanding its volcanic surface, is in many places a land of green pastures and fat farms, while the barren shores of Greenland are buried under almost perpetual ice and snow." While gazing on this panorama, still very early in the day, I was joined by a companion, Prince Arnolph of Bavaria, first cousin to the present King, who, with his elder brother Prince Leopold-Maximilian was intending to visit Iceland, and now declared, as he came on deck, this first appearance of the coast to be superior to any thing he had seen previously, surpassing even that view of the Alps upon the Continent from the Cathedral of Milan, owing to the sea which lay between.

In five hours after this we put in at Djupivogr, on the Beru Fjord, under a scorching sun, which was overpowering on board ship, and compelled some to seek for shelter ; while the prevalence of N.E. wind will probably account for the snow still being left upon the mountains in this quarter, and not upon the W. or S. at all, except inland. Another reason for the absence for all ice or snow upon the west side of the island is the presence of the Gulf stream, which keeps all the ports of Iceland open in winter, while we hear of Copenhagen, Christiania, and Stockholm being frozen up. At the place above mentioned where we first put in, being on the east coast, there is no Gulf stream : so that on forming a hasty conclusion, any one might easily consider Iceland deserving of its name. I mention Djupivogr, where we did not land, as it helps one to comprehend the great size of this island (somewhat larger than Ireland), since our voyage from here by steam along the coast continued all that day and the whole day after. Similar to Arabia, the interior of Iceland is a trackless desert and uninhabited, but in some places covered with good pasture, although barren for the most part, and consisting of whole plains of lava for ever swept with flying dust and sand. The view which now succeeded was one continuation of chaotic masses, evidently turned up by some earthquake, all barren, desolate, and black. There is no harbour on the whole south coast, nor any place of shelter for the numerous French fishing smacks and whalers that come here in summer-time, except Eyrabakki, for the beach is inaccessible along the whole intermediate space between this place and Beru Fjord, owing to the heavy swell and absence of outlying islands or rocks to break it.

On the second day there was considerable excitement, when, touching at that little group of islands (about twenty miles from the mainland)

called Vestmannas, from the West men, that
is to say, the Irishmen, who went out as ancho-
rites, and lived here in seclusion (like Saint
Senanus) long before the Norsemen had ever
discovered such a place. These islands, if we
may so call them, have only one habitable part,
a village and some meadow, while the whole
appearance of the group, as seen from the mainland, is a mere cluster of isolated crags and dark
cliffs, perpetually whitened .by the spray, and as
if they had formerly been in one mass, but by
some earthquake had since fallen asunder. Between these cliffs and precipices we now passed,
and it would be hard to name another place on
earth with so great and dense a congregation of
wild sea-birds of every variety; puffins, auks, and
sea-mews, drawn up in rows on every ledge, each
kind on a ledge to itself, as if to do us honour;
but when an experiment was tried upon them by
firing one of the ship's guns, and the sound of
cannon was answered by the flapping of millions

of wings, scarcely could anything in nature be more extraordinary; and, as the sound was again and again reverberated, as the echo of this cannon sounded among other cliffs, the immeasurable multitude of birds that got up, as rising and spreading clouds, for some seconds darkened the air.

Daylight continued at this period of the year so long, that when the time of night came on, and it might have been four in the afternoon, a clock would make it eleven in the evening. Twilight began at twelve, and often have I, when on shore at midnight, started on a ramble during the "inexplicable stillness" between twelve and two, when the sensation was that of being on some other planet in broad twilight, with all nature wrapt in silence—moors, brushwood, every twig all motionless as death, and perhaps not a cloud upon the sky. So it was upon this evening, the last night at sea, when having gone right round the south coast of Iceland we entered

Faxa Fjord upon the west, and anchored about half-past two in front of Reikjavik the following morning. On landing a few hours after this, the princes and I were welcomed by the Governor, and invited to a ball for Saturday, July 20 (the very day after), at his residence, a whitewashed house, built of lava. Here, by the way, I would recommend for the convenience of all future travellers,—take an evening suit, and may they have the same opportunity to wear it and may it come in as useful as did mine. The princes had theirs also, and went in it, but did not dance. With regard to the dress of the ladies, I speak only of those who wore the native Icelandic costume, it resembled a white robe, and might have been of any material; the ornament of the head being in shape like a helmet, and white also, similar to what we see upon the statues of Minerva, so great is the antiquity of it, and worn, I am told, only in one part of the world besides Iceland, that from which the race must have

originally come—Circassia: especially if it be
true that Odin, father of the Scandinavian race,
and deity of their religion, was chieftain of a
Scythian tribe, as we read in the heroic ages of
their history. Above the forehead are four or five
silver-gilt stars, and a white muslin veil thrown
back; one other graceful article not worn by all,
is a belt round the waist, of massive silver, divided
in tablets with figures and designs all cut in high
relief. Such is the costume on their state occa-
sions, and such it was on this; the Government
House rooms were thrown open and lighted up
with tallow candles in wooden chandeliers, to
prevent which from being blown out was probably one reason why the windows were all closed,
making the place so warm that many wished the
ball might have taken place by Arctic twilight
and out of doors instead. The music was provided by a naval band from a Danish sloop then
lying in the harbour, of which the officers also,
towards the end, became musical themselves,

singing songs in chorus as they stood after a
supper, to which we all sat down while his
excellency the governor favoured us with an
address. I thought there was more beauty of
feature in Iceland than in Norway (from last
year's experience), that the Icelanders were a finer
race, and on making some such remark to an
Icelander the day afterwards he said, " We are in
this country a royal race; descended from no
common lot of colonists and settlers, but from
those exiled kings and their families who left
Norway a thousand years ago, in deep determination they would not submit to the supremacy of
Harold Harfager, who had usurped their thrones.
And our pedigrees in some cases may be traced
without a break, even to that epoch." I suppose
no other country of this present world of Europe,
Asia, Africa, or America, has been colonised at the
outset by emigrants of that stamp, whatever may
have been the nature of their royalty.

On the following morning we attended the

cathedral service and mingled with the congregation, who appeared to be chiefly of the poorer
class, but joined famously in all the music and
responses, most of which is the same as in the
churches of Copenhagen, or wherever the
Lutheran religion has spread; but some of the
Icelandic music has a character unlike that of
other nations: for instance, a hymn composed at
the national festival to commemorate the settlement of the island for a thousand years, and sung
last year with great effect in this very cathedral;
it was declared in the words of the *Times* correspondent, "even by Swedish connoisseurs, to be
a masterly composition of its kind. The choir
of male and female voices mixed was singularly
impressive, and every foreigner to whom I spoke
coming out bore witness to the exceedingly
devotional and tender character of the singing,
and the corresponding behaviour of the congregation." Of *national songs* belonging to this
country many are very remarkable, especially that

which celebrates the arrival of the plover in early spring, since that event invariably heralds the breaking up of winter, and approach of ships from other lands ; one might hear this in chorus of an evening but not in Reikjavik, only up the country, where they reap the benefit of intercourse with other lands without being influenced by foreigners. At Reikjavik one may hear great variety in music, especially of Danish, Swedish, and Norwegian composition ; but none appeared so totally distinct (of all their foreign songs) as a piece they had from Finland, sung one day by a party with the Governor of Iceland at the Geysers in the desert, by his guides and mine, called in the language of Finland " Suomis." To return to the cathedral, one need only mention in the way of art, that it contains a very beautiful baptismal font, shaped like a square pedestal with figures in relief upon each side, made by the great Thorvaldsen, and presented to this country where his family had lived

for generations, his name also being Icelandic,
while he himself was born upon the sea between
here and Copenhagen, not in Denmark as is
usually supposed. No other historic interest has
attached to the present cathedral, it was only
built in the beginning of this century, and yet
the stones of it have shown signs already of
crumbling away; but within its precincts are
a good museum and a library, which I had the
honour by the way of visiting in company with
that great traveller Captain Burton, who was out
this year and making observations with regard to
the extensive mineral wealth (as I understood)
which undoubtedly lies hidden in this country.
He said it was established now beyond a doubt—
what all the same the Icelanders would reject with
scorn—as a piece of ethnology, that descendants
of the Esquimaux race were certainly seen sometimes in Iceland, chiefly to be recognised (if I
remember right) by their hair, even more than
by the colour of their skin. On the following

morning, the princes having tried some horses made a start, intending to go round the island by the north, so we agreed to set off in opposite directions, while I, with ten horses, two for guides, two more for tent and baggage, and a reserve of five to be exchanged upon the journey at every four hours, made at once for Hecla.

There is a tradition that, upon a certain mountain in some part of Ireland, "the ghosts of persons who have died in foreign lands walk about and converse with those they meet, like living people" and when asked by any who have known them in life why they return not to their homes, give all the same answer alike, declare they must return to Mount Hecla in Iceland, and vanish instantly. Moore in his Irish Melodies has made these beings wish they might taste life again, thus giving answer—

" And ere condemned we go, to freeze 'mid Hecla's snow,
  We would taste it awhile, and think we live once more."

However that may be, I saw, with no slight

melancholy and heaviness, this far-renowned
volcano so near the Arctic circle, the first sight
of which now called to mind the desolations it
has spread over this region far and wide, at
various periods of Iceland's history, averaging
three eruptions in a century for the past 800
years. To change the subject, it would be difficult to find a more obliging, experienced, and
honest man than my head guide; he bore a
name that all will recognise who have ever been
this way, Geir Zöega, and wherever I went, his
countrymen received him with great cordiality.
In addition to his ordinary employment, this
man had frequently undertaken expeditions for
the capture of the Iceland falcon, a *variety* of
the ger falcon, in consequence of hawking
having been revived upon the continent, as in
Belgium and Holland, where it has been introduced from Denmark; and the Iceland falcon,
being superior to the peregrine both in docility
and strength, is held in great demand. But our

man will not **bargain** for two falcons, nor even three, as nets have **to** be spread and taken into such barren, **remote places, that** twenty is the smallest number **to** make **it** worth his while. Stories that he used to tell **me of** danger and difficulties in **the** pursuit, served **to** pass the time on horseback when traversing a dreary region.

"*Monday, July* 22.—Started **on** horseback at 9.30 with Zöega and Einar, **for Hecla.** Reached Laugardoelir at 8.30 P.M.—40 **miles."** At first everything **shone** bright, and various circumstances **gave to our** journey something of an **Oriental tinge, what with a** burning sun and shifting sand, while the procession of our horses (like a caravan) **kept in single file.** I saw the mirage in the distance, like **a sheet** of water, clear enough and **glittering, but hazy;** vanishing at **the first cloud over the sun, it then** gave place to shifting pillars **of loose sand,** caught in some whirlwind, **or in many,** apparently connecting earth and sky! **This day** our cavalcade went

over forty miles, **and we did** that in eleven hours,
which gave to **next** morning all the benefit of a
good start, and left nothing whatever to complain
of but the heat, on account **of which some**
people invariably travel by night, there being
scarcely any darkness at this time of year. **No**
time had been lost upon that distance, although
as a rule the people of Iceland fail quite to
understand the value **of it,** and resemble society
in the East by an extent **of conversation the**
whole day, when there is apparently nothing whatever to discuss. The night was spent in **a farm-**
house rich in its quantity and **quality of milk**
and cream, **we** having entered **now** within the
boundary of human habitations, and left the
desert for a land **of** pasture, which bore every
appearance of **prosperity,** and was enlivened by
the sight of people getting in their hay; this
"hay time" **is** their harvest, the one great **crop**
of the country, in which **their wealth** consists.
It may **be as** well **to** mention **the name of this**

farm (though not of much use to the general
eader) was Laugardoelir, since by stopping here
the first night we were able to arrive at (or very
near to) the foot of Hecla on the second day,
continuing our route along the banks of a great
river without any variety hour after hour, until
there came a chance of crossing it—in the way all
rivers throughout Iceland, if of any considerable
size, have to be crossed, by driving in the horses
first, and following with every bit of baggage in a
boat, while they swim to the shore opposite and
we follow in pursuit, now and then cracking a
whip; when fairly out of their depth and obliged
to struggle hard against the river, we soon see
nothing but their heads, which keep however in
a group, and want no guiding where to go.   In
this country there are no bridges, **and** the rivers
exceed **those of great** Britain in length, so they
have always to **be** forded, in which case the horses
feel their ground **with very** remarkable skill,
never making a false step, even in water of a thick

white colour (of which **these rivers** generally
are) and anything **but** transparent; **while one**
has to give a **horse his head and not attempt to**
guide him, or it will **soon be over with both**
horse and man. The height of **these horses may**
be from 11 **to** 13 hands, and their **worth from**
150 to 280 rix-dalers, from 17*l.* **to** 31*l.* sterling:
a pack-horse **will cost from** 5*l.* **to** 10*l.*, but **vary**
according to the **year; a great** exodus **of** horses
took place **this** very season, several **shiploads,**
each of 300 **or** 400 horses at **once,** left **this**
country, **no doubt for the mines in** England.
With regard to **our journey, the afternoon of that**
second day **found us after** five **and thirty miles**
(our horses being all the better **for the** water) **at**
Storuvellir, **a comfortable** wooden house covered
outside with **sod, the** dwelling **of** a Lutheran
minister, in full view of the great Hecla, which
next morning—if weather permitted—I, with **the**
minister's son, **Gudmundr, and second guide**
Einar Sœmundsson, had **made out a plan to**

ascend; the head guide, before mentioned, now
declined, on the ground of it not being his business ! because the horses took up all his care, for
one reason; but no Icelander ever dared the
ascent until shown the way by Sir Joseph Banks,
or ever accomplished it until he came, and
even now the oldest inhabitants appear to have
superstitious notions concerning it.

So it happened the next morning at a little
after ten, when the sun was shining brightly but
obscured by clouds, that only the three of us got
under way : myself upon a horse generously
offered by the worthy minister to give the other
ones a rest, a cob in which he took great pride.
An hour and a half brought us easily to
Noefrholt, a farmhouse that will be the first to
perish in the next violent eruption of this mountain, the last one having been in '45, but only of
moderate extent, as Noetrholt is a dwelling-place
of greater antiquity by far. At this spot there
appeared to be a very unnecessary delay, some

local guide was wanted who knew the mountain, and until he came the time was spent in sorting various old manuscripts on paper that were found within this lonely habitation ; on which the family depended for whatever they would have in winter to occupy their minds. We ordered at the same time some coffee, which was ground and roasted for us on the spot, and proved so exhilarating that the present writer at once cleared a hedge in front of the house upon the strength of it, followed by Gudmundr in quick succession, who alighted at the same moment with all decorum and without altering his countenance.

Such as the reverence shown by Egyptians to the Nile, or felt by Germans for the Rhine, was the veneration manifested for Mount Hecla by this young man; it had always been opposite his home, and called out this very feeling in all he said or did, when anywhere within its neighbour-hood. We began the ascent about twelve, by

riding, for two hours more, so far up as the
horses would go safely, since travelling on foot
in Iceland is accounted very mean.   Leaving the
horses at the end of that time, we began to
ascend in earnest, but soon afterwards became
enveloped in a regular white mist—which made
the local guide from Noefrholt commence presently to look about him, so as to show us every
now and then, smiling, an unmistakably fine
set of teeth.   " Fog," says the Icelandic proverb,
"is a beautiful king's daughter, veiled in spells :
she will be freed from them, only when all
shepherds and mountaineers shall agree in *blessing* her."   This is like saying that whenever the
so-called " organ " upon the face of the cliff
at the Giant's Causeway shall begin to play, the
whole natural curiosity will turn round three
times : or that whenever, and directly, the ruined
palace of Ballyscullion, close to Lough Beg in the
county of Londonderry, is restored, the Duke of
Connaught will come there to reside.   To return

to our present situation, **the compass proved**
entirely useless, by reason of some iron, most
likely, in the mountain; **and our footing more-**
over was by no means sure, **any more than on**
the ashes of Vesuvius; **while the surrounding**
scene was at this crisis like some **vast remains of**
a smouldering fire, only just extinguished, **its**
ashes and cinders **all fresh, black, loose, and of**
great size, while the mist rolled **in between them.**
Here for a time **we remained** standing, not
knowing whither to proceed; our bearings were
entirely lost, nor did we **make them out until**
Einar Sœmundsson (second guide) discovered on
the ashes very near to where we stood a *footprint*
—which was proved afterwards to be **that of**
Captain Burton (or one **of his party this year)—**
and we followed the direction **of it right on to**
the summit, arriving about five **o'clock upon the**
brink of that narrow crater, made **by the last**
eruption. Down into **this we now crept upon**
the ice **and** snow, in very humble **attitude, the**

others allowing me—with all due ceremony—to
go first. Presently the opening admitted only a
limited supply of light: so finding we had gained
a place where it was possible to stand upright,
and hoping there might be some extraordinary
echo, I called a halt and made the others chant
a national air, one that was of great antiquity;
the song went off very well, but the echo was
disappointing. Coming out again into the light,
each one of us took part in that ode of Horace
—for the Icelanders know Latin—which has
been set to music by a man named Flemming,
and commences—

> "Integer vitæ scelerisque purus, ...
> Sive per Syrtes iter æstuosas,
> Sive facturus per *inhospitalem*
> *Caucasum,* vel quæ loca fabulosus
> Lambit Hydaspes,"

which the connection between the Caucasus
and Iceland, before alluded to, might tempt
one to change into *Hyperborean latitudes* if
the ode were English, or into *Hyperboreos*

montes if it were another metre, " an imaginary range of mountains in the N. of the **Earth,** afterwards applied **by** geographers to various chains, as for example—The Caucasus."

We scraped away a little of **the snow beneath** our feet, then made a slight hollow **in the earth,** and the heat of the stones resembled that of **red-** hot coals, no easy **matter** to lay hold of, **even at** this short distance from the surface ; then as the mist showed **no** sign of clearing up or letting us have any of that view so magnificent in fine weather, I agreed we should descend—but did not see the reason of such violent haste as the others now began to show in making for their horses. I was borne along **in** the confusion, and **sadly** began to feel (by the way these fellows went on) the force of that old established saying, standard proverb, and **wise** maxim, that

" An old man in love, is like Mount Hecla: the summit is covered with snow, while the inside is full of flame !"

Gudmundr, whose name has occurred already

as a companion, continued so throughout the
time I spent upon the island : whether receiving
or returning the hospitality of Reikjavik, whether
travelling by land, or going anywhere by sea—
in town he shared my lodging, at sea my cabin,
and on land my tent. His attainments made
him of great service in explaining the literature and language of the people throughout
Iceland, as he knew the old language naturally,
and spoke excellent English besides, having
been at the college of Reikjavik, and there made
good use of his time ; explaining to me also, by
his knowledge of past history, everything upon
the route : for the usages of the present day
in Iceland are the same as they have been for
centuries, and many a humble dwelling that we
passed was inhabited by a family that dated
back as far, if we are to believe them, as the
time which the Sagas describe. Not more than
twenty years of age, Gudmundr possessed features
of that pure Norman type that we occasionally

see in an old portrait, enough to remind any
one that Normandy and Iceland were colonized
from the same source, while the more his young
countrymen approached him in resemblance, the
better looking they appeared to be.   His mother
came of an old family, by name Thorarinnson,
members of which have in Denmark and at
home held various offices of state ; and, to notice
a circumstance in the domestic customs of this
country, he the second son was sent to college to
prepare for public life, while his elder brother
stayed at home without the benefit of education
to take care of their father's farm, and in the end
succeed to it, which was thought more honour-
able.   The present writer, having found no
difficulty in the Danish language, had opportunities of seeing and understanding this people
which the ordinary traveller tied for time does
not obtain ; and had the experiences then gained
only been written down before, these pages might
have been a little more diffuse.

Having ordered our caravan on the following
morning to be in readiness for a visit to Skalholt,
the whole party, consisting now of four—one
more by the addition of Gudmundr—set off in
good order, and first had to traverse an immense
extent of plain, chiefly pasture, and of a refreshing greenness, passing in sight of that singular
mountain, called, in allusion to its shape,
Jarlhatten (the Earl's cap), which formed, with
other mountains, a complete but remote panorama
till we came to Hruni, leaving one free to enjoy
that expanse of level plain, and gallop with un-
bounded ecstasy far ahead of the retinue sometimes.   At Hruni there lived another minister,
the Lutheran archdeacon over all other ministers
in this part of Iceland, whose name was Briem,
and whose family were said to be remarkable for
the size and brightness of their eyes. Having
paid him a visit, and been very courteously
received, the journey was continued to Skalholt,
the site of an ancient cathedral, for two hours and

a half more. By this time "the peculiar blue which in Iceland settles upon, and softens down, distant mountain views, seemed now to envelop the whole horizon in a veil of slumbering peacefulness," and we spent the evening at a heap of large stones, called, in Icelandic, "Scola varda" (schoolboy leisure), the only memorial to point out where a celebrated college flourished once—a heap of stones which has been imitated by the present college, now near Reikjavik, and called by the same name, to pass the time of its industrious young students, if ever they have any to spare. With regard to the old cathedral, now become an ordinary parish church, I saw no less than twelve tombstones upon the floor, several of great age, some bearing inscriptions in Latin, some in Icelandic, each cut into the stone so deep as to be distinctly legible; and they spread my mattress on a bishop's grave, one Finnr Jónsson, according to a custom of this country, whereby a traveller may pass the night in

church, without **disrespect to a** religious edifice
or desecration of a holy place; therefore, like the
Spirit of Solitude, speaking to his parent, Nature,
in the words of Shelley:

> " I have made my bed
> In charnels and on coffins, where black Death
> Keeps record of the trophies won from thee;
> Hoping to still these obstinate questionings
> Of thee and thine, by forcing some **lone** ghost,
> Thy messenger, to render up the tale
> **Of what we are."**

So slept the living with the dead, but woke again
when sunrise came from over miles and miles
of level, far-extending plain, when it began **to**
stream **in by the window;** I stretched, rose up,
and, as it were in grave clothes—without dressing
beforehand, stood to behold it from the ruinous
churchyard.

Before **we leave the sacred spot,** there is a
history it has in common with two or three
ancient bishoprics much nearer home, for, in the
days when Scotland **was more or** less under the
dominion of Norway, the bishopric of Kirkwall

in Orkney, of Sodor (Iona) and **Man, of Skalholt**
as well as **of** Holar, in Iceland, **were included**
within the archbishopric of Trondhjem.   **There**
is now of all Iceland but one bishop, and **of**
Trondhjem no archbishop; but the bishop of
Trondhjem still possesses the right of placing
the crown upon the king's head, in a **cathedral**
where all the kings of Norway and Sweden **have**
been crowned, and where Nicholas Breakspear,
in the twelfth century, **when upon** his missionary
journey to Scandinavia under **Pope** Eugene III.,
in all probability had something to **say.**   I en-
close a sketch of this ancient edifice, drawn **and**
given me in Iceland by a lady.

This day, within three hours **from Skalholt, we**
pitched our tent at the celebrated Geysers (pronounced like Gazer) **or Hot** Springs, arriving
there about noon; **distance in** this country, as in
India, being reckoned entirely by time.   Situated
in a sandy desert, **I found** the neighbourhood of
these hot springs decidedly what would be called

by the credulous, especially in Ireland, a "gentle
place." There is something in the air about it
which is uncanny, which comes over the spirits
like a sweet poison, enough to make the most
hard-hearted person easy going and good tem-
pered for a while. Who should arrive in less
than half an hour, but the governor of Iceland
himself, accompanied by Mrs. Finsen his lady,
and her brother from Denmark, with a whole
retinue, conveying all they might require for an
absence of five or six days, journey included, from
the capital. Having raised our hats, saluted him,
and waited till each of his party had been able
to dismount, we led the way to that lesser spring,
called the Strokr, which can be made to play at
any time by proper management. Having heard
beforehand that his Excellency might be expected, I had provided here, at the suggestion of
Einar Sœmundsson (who detected the footprint of
Captain Burton on Mount Hecla), a wheelbarrow
of turf—every bit of which had to be paid for,

because it contained pasture—off the ground; this was now tumbled into the well, so as to produce a display of this fountain for the governor's honour, and very soon was followed by a rumbling sound (the fountain was in labour) preparatory to the sending up a whole column of scalding water, which rose to a great height above our heads. It was at first intended that we should display the willing fountain at the moment when the governor's party might appear in sight, but, not knowing what kind of impression this might produce upon his horses, I thought better to wait until he came.

So then we returned to the edge of the Great Geyser's basin, near to which both tents had been pitched, side by side. All parties were obliged to wait upon the caprice of this natural wonder, the monster fountain seldom caring now to play; no stones or earth can be thrown in to draw it out, under a penalty of 900 rix-dalers (£100), and it has been known for travellers to live here a whole

week, without seeing it put forth its power. As
time went on we made some tea, filling our kettles
with that boiling water which was ready on all
sides, from twenty springs at least, but some of
only moderate extent. It soon occurred to us,
all the same, that, however refreshing might be
the tea, a very small quantity of the water went a
considerable way, and that, to get accustomed to
it, would be to give one's inside a thin coating all
round, something like those charming cameos
which are to be had in Italy, from the mineral
waters at Vichy. So by way of an employment
next morning, I spent a long time in collecting,
and at last brought in upon a plate, some different
specimens of petrifaction—sticks, grass, moss,
all bleached and coated over with hard stone;
especially beautiful, moreover, were the leaves
that (blown here somehow) lay spread out white
upon the soil, very dazzling in the sunshine, like
some new fossil, and always entire, but as fragile,
delicate and brittle as the shell of any nautilus

inside. These were acceptable to Mrs. Finsen,
the same of whom it was written by the *Times*
correspondent at the festival last year, that upon
the arrival of His Majesty of Denmark, " In a very
homely but exceedingly graceful manner," she
" came down the steps leading up the terrace to
the entrance, and bade her sovereign and guest
' many times welcome.' "

But it was during the first night, while a strict
watch was being kept, and orders had been given
to arouse the encampment if any symptoms of
eruption were either felt or heard, that, between
two and three o'clock A.M., or thereabouts, I
began to feel an inclination of the ground to
be unsteady, sleeping at the time on a kind of
mattress within the tent and very soundly, yet
woke up all at once by what was unmistakably a
gentle shaking of the earth, making our watch
unnecessary. Gudmundr evidently felt the same.
We were just about to ask each other for an
explanation, when outside was heard a loud

clapping of hands—summoning every one to
behold this gigantic, unexplained, weird miracle
of nature by the light of the rising sun, in full
glory! Imagine a column of sparkling water
playing up to the height of eighty or a hundred
feet, which last was the height agreed on at the
time, and so large in circumference as the steam
around its base would allow any one to perceive!
clouds of thick, pure white, and heavy steam
hung round it, while the spray above shone glittering like thousands, like millions of diamonds,
before the sun. It will easily be understood we
slept no more that morning; the deepest feelings
of wonder at so much of majesty and such display of power kept us wide awake henceforward,
and upon the stretch. Nor did fortune even then
desert us, for in the course of that same day we
saw the sparkling monster four times more; less
and less high each succeeding time, but always
a satisfactory performance. And among the
wonders of this place I must not neglect to

mention a perfect bath, which after every
eruption of the Geyser is filled with tepid water
in a flowing stream, and contains ledges which
resemble seats. The boiling water which escapes
from the great Geyser's basin flows over a cold
slab of rock in this particular direction, and
falls at last over the edge, where in course of
time it has scooped out this hollow; the sides
and seats, all natural, are tinged by the mineral
quality of the water with a kind of rosy hue;
and in some places by a reddish yellow, where
the earth itself is like a hard and sparkling sand-
stone, while the seats and edges have all been
rounded off by the action of this water, which
poured, as Gudmundr and I sat in the bath,
upon our heads.

Early on Sunday morning the governor's party
broke up the encampment. Their tent when
I awoke had disappeared; and then I recollected
(being more or less perhaps half stupid from
the atmosphere) that we really did part the

previous evening after supper all on the very best
of terms, in hearty conviviality.   Gudmundr also
having left me on a visit somewhere in the
neighbourhood, arranging we should meet the
following day upon the road, I yielded to the
fascination of this "gentle place," and waited here
in sleepy solitude until the sun went down, wishing
to travel for a change by night, when we folded
our tent "like the Arab, and as silently stole
away."

Commencing the night journey to Thingvalla,
we made a considerable circuit in order to see
the remains of a Pagan temple mentioned in the
story of Burnt Njal, now called Hof, but for the
ancient name I recommend any one to that
excellent translation, by Dasent, of the above
story. Nothing but mounds and a rounded
hollow in the earth remain now to be seen.
Returning therefore through a number of
people from a neighbouring farmhouse who
wondered what we had come to see, the track

was soon regained, and led us for some height above the plain, passing in the distance a bright sheet of water, concerning which Geir Zöega told me the following mysterious story: That three young men, Icelanders, once went in here to bathe, and each entering the water at the same moment were seen all at once to disappear (by some one from a distance) and rise no more above the surface; on his coming to the place, their bodies were found lying in less than five feet deep of water, just where they had sunk out of sight, without any appearance of having struggled for life, and where it was impossible they could have been drowned. The only explanation ever given was that some electric eel, or creature of that kind, which alone is able to produce these fearful effects upon any animal that may come in contact with it, lived and writhed in the bottom of this lonely lake—known by the name of Apavatn. The way led over wide and level slabs of rock, as we continued this

desolate and gloomy journey, travelling for the first
time by night; and as a specimen of the *roads*
in Iceland, this one here became a deep track
in the solid rock from twelve to eighteen inches
wide, neatly rounded on both sides, worn by
nothing but the horses' feet which have been this
way for centuries; to prove the antiquity of these
thoroughfares, I have seen sometimes a pile of
stones to mark the place where some one has
been murdered, as many were in former days, left
still by the roadside where it had been heaped up
600 years ago—when the road was in constant
use day after day.

Presently there appeared before us a great
sheet of water some way farther on, dimly visible
in the shadowy half-light which already had succeeded the bright twilight of an earlier season.
This was Thingvalla, the largest lake in Iceland,
so celebrated in the past. My own impressions,
on first seeing this distinctly, were that I had
seen it before: an island in the centre, another

one toward the side, a promontory, every winding
of the shore, each part of it, the whole scene
struck me as familiar, and as if in some previous
existence I had visited and dwelt upon the spot,
or recollected living there and had known it
from a child.   We find a similar experience in
the life of Charles Dickens, who describes it on
his first sight of Ferrara: " On the foreground
was a group of silent peasant girls leaning over
the parapet of a little bridge, looking now up at
the sky now down into the water; in the distance
a deep bell; the shadow of approaching night on
everything.   If I had been murdered there in
some former life I could not have seemed to
remember the place more thoroughly, or with
more emphatic chilling of the blood; and the
real remembrance of it acquired in that minute
is so strengthened by the imaginary recollection,
that I scarcely think I could forget it."

We arrived at the glebe house of the present
minister, having nearly parted company in the

darkness more than once upon the way, between huge boulders which made it very hard to keep together in some places; but after rallying in single file upon a better road towards the end, our horses very soon came to the present church, close to the dwelling of its minister, before which, not liking to disturb him, we once more spread our tent.

At breakfast in his house next morning there was some conversation between us upon the ancient constitution of the country, for it was here the Icelanders in olden time used all to meet for the promulgation of their laws, in the days of their former Republic. This assembly was called the Althing. It had powers legislative and judiciary. Breakfast over, I was introduced to the different localities upon the plain, shown where this open-air parliament had met in past ages, and where each department of the government was formerly transacted. Not to continue here any longer than is necessary, or treat the situation as a

piece of holy ground, going into the customary
transport of Republican enthusiasm,* I would
call attention to a very sensible remark by one
of the farmer deputies present at the introduction
of the new form of government last year upon
this very place, when it was a matter of discus-
sion how they were to receive Christian IX., *the
first king who ever reigned in Iceland,* and
some proposed to receive him with expressions of
general gratitude for the new constitution that
he brought, while others murmured and thought
that would be to over-estimate the benefit; a
farmer deputy sent by one of the electoral dis-
tricts, said, " Whatever you do you must not
flatter or speak falsely before our king. This
people has done so much already to assert their
right to the full enjoyment of liberty, that it
would ill become us were we so little hearted
before our sovereign as not to have the honesty

* " Exit in a transport of philanthropical enthusiasm, kicks the
Knife-grinder, and overturns his wheel."

to tell him of our sincere love to himself and of
our determination to make the constitution,
which is now demonstrably a very imperfect
instrument, one by which the gift which his
majesty has given to us can be made worthy of
the name of a boon. His majesty shall have
from us only that which we desire from him—
love from our hearts and truth from our lips;
such, it seems to me, the people of Iceland should
always show to the world. It was the wont of
our forefathers; the custom is not yet so anti-
quated as to deserve to be given up. I am much
mistaken in the king if he desires from us fine
phrases rather than the straightforward language
which conveys to him the straightforward mind
of his faithful subjects." I am indebted to the
Times correspondent for a translation of this
into English from the Icelandic original. The
address which they decided on was given two
days afterwards, and "began by wishing His
Majesty welcome to the country, and by express-

ing the hope that his majesty's visit to Iceland
might be one which coming generations would
cherish. While the people of Iceland must
regret—the address went on—that his majesty's
eye should rest everywhere upon the results of
the Danish government of past ages—poverty
and misery—it was a matter of congratulation
for ruler and ruled that there lingered still,
despite long troubles and severe trials, in the
heart of the nation, the old manhood and en-
durance. The Icelandic nation had never been
so determined as now, when the rays of the
general civilization of the world had begun to
dawn upon the people by their more free and
frequent intercourse with other countries, to
assert its right to an Icelandic national existence,
the ideal purpose of which should be the steady
development of the people in every direction,
intellectual and material." Having been favoured
with an old copy of the *Times*, I find that as
the king rode away at the conclusion of the

national meeting, "nearly the whole of the
assembled crowds of Thingvalla ranged themselves on both sides of the road, in order to give
His Majesty one more farewell cheer." It is
very gratifying to an English mind, considering
the tender relationship of His Majesty to our
Princess of Wales, to hear that "with truth
Iceland never saw a more welcome guest; his
dignified bearing, his ready affability and wonderfully winning manners and unassuming simplicity, are qualities which have won for him the
whole heart of the people." Amid the demon-
strations of affection to King Christian IX., "close
to the road on the left, a little in front of the
spot where his majesty was to stop to listen to the
address of welcome, were stationed twenty-four
young maidens in Icelandic dress," like priestesses
of old, "with flowers ready to strew in His
Majesty's path as soon as he should move on
after the greeting." Among the ships of different
nations in the harbour of Reikjavik that had

come to do honour to the occasion, was a man-of-war from Norway, the mother country, " with a deputation on board of Norwegian students, littérateurs and poets, the latter sent by order of King Oscar of Sweden." To represent this European power there is a consul, as popular as he is well known, Mr. Siemsen; there being also a consul for the French, and a consul for the Dutch, all three resident in Reikjavik. But to represent English interests there is no resident authority, while the number of British vessels employed in fishing round this coast, to mention but one kind of trade here carried on, makes that to be a want often felt; and at many places with which England has far less to do than Reikjavik, there is an English consul. It was remarked on the occasion of the late festival, that England, the nearest neighbour to Iceland, had sent no ship, while France, Sweden, Denmark, and Norway, each sent one ship at least; moreover, to represent each of these powers, there is now a resident authority; England continues to withhold acknowledgment from a constitutional entity of political Europe, increasing in commerce, prosperity and power day by day, while the alliance of royalty with Denmark only makes that omission all the more extraordinary. When the late administration, indifferent to foreign policy, omitted, with great want of attention, to send even a single ship to represent England at the coronation of His Majesty King Oscar II. in Stockholm, they had the wisdom, on discovering the mistake, to send not only five men-of-war to the coronation afterwards at Trondhjem, albeit secondary in importance, but also a Prince of the blood, whose presence atoned quickly for the error. May we not in this case hope the present government will make up for an omission by appointing some one to represent us, will amend this piece of foreign policy, and discontinue the anomaly of there being no resident authority, without any more delay?

CHAPTER II.

ICELAND.

" And from **wrecks** of ships, and drifting
Spars, uplifting
On the desolate, **rainy seas,**
* * * *

Ever drifting, drifting, drifting
On the shifting
Currents of the restless main;
Till in sheltered coves, and reaches
Of sandy beaches,
All **have found repose again.**"

ETURNING then to Reikjavik, upon the road occurred an instance of that wise and **happy custom,** whereby all whom it may concern **ride out** from that metropolis to **meet** the **governor.** I overtook him where he lay encamped, upon an oasis called

Selgadalr, some way out of town; where, for
his reception, they had spread an extensive picnic,
to which I was also invited: and when all had
partaken of the wine from Copenhagen, the ladies,
who had acted the part of servants, according to
the custom of this country, and of cup-bearers,
cleared away the things. Horses were ordered,
the whole party mounted, and then, to all appearance, began the journey home; but this was not
the case, although our journey lay in that
direction, for, by-and-by, the order was given
to draw up at a well-to-do farmhouse, dismount,
and take some coffee.

I well remember the conversation turning upon
reindeer, which exist in Iceland, but are very
rarely seen—in fact, are only to be found in two
corners of the island, south-west, and north-east.
And even these are not indigenous to the country,
having been, originally, brought over by someone
from Norway, and let loose, while no one ever
thinks of going out to look for reindeer, and any

farmer, who may chance to meet with buck or
doe upon his land, will have no peace till he has
killed the same, and saved his sheep from their
imaginary danger. Nor do they ever harness the
animal in this country. There is no such thing
as a tame reindeer in Iceland; only in Lapland,
or some parts of Sweden—quite another region
of the globe. Speaking of the use of reindeer in
a sledge, Moore says:

> "I saw the moon rise clear,
>   O'er hills and vales of snow,
> Nor taught my fleet reindeer
>   The path he was to go.
> But quick he bounded forth,
>   For well my reindeer knew
> I've but one path on earth—
>   The path that leads to you!"

A pair of tame reindeer were offered to me
once for 20 dalers, Norwegian (£4 10s. or so),
but not until long after this. As for the Lap-
landers, their whole wealth consists in reindeer,
and to drive them, a piece of rope is fastened to
each horn, by the gentleman, who then gets into

the sledge and guides them, in that manner, where to go.

Setting off again we got into a good gallop, every horse being familiar with the road, and arrived at Reikjavik about 9 P.M., previous to which I picked up Gudmundr at the place agreed upon the other day. Etiquette has laid it down upon these riding parties, that the whole number on horseback shall escort each other home, stopping at the different houses as they pass, till the whole party, and only in order of their rank, have been deposited in safety. We came in by the east end of the town, passed between houses all semi-detached, with geraniums or fuchsias in every window, while the whole appearance of the place manifested great cleanliness and care. With a population of between two and three thousand only, this bright and healthy little capital " is well laid out into streets, while the social circles *of the better sort* indicate a refinement and happiness, which might be envied in more civilized places of

the globe." The day following, myself and
Gudmundr resolved to rest upon our oars, and
began that festive mode of life, to be received from
house to house, in which the good people of
Reikjavik show welcome to a stranger, to the
weatherbound or captive traveller, laid up in port.
For general intelligence, the inhabitants of Reikjavik are equal to any capital in Europe, and I
shall ever remember their kind attention during
the whole period of my stay. As to the mode of
visiting, people's cards were often to be found
pinned on my front door—since the houses of
Reikjavik have neither bell nor knocker!—and
the letters of introduction which I took appeared
not to be wanted after all. In the streets at night,
there is a likeness to Pompeii, arctic twilight
blending with the same " inexplicable stillness ;"
and the apartments I occupied were in the centre
of the town, looking out upon that open space
behind, called Austrovellir ; while in front, was a
view of the sea. The anchorage is good, and the

bay defended from heavy seas by several small
islands, which render it a safe harbour. The appearance of Reikjavik is happy and bright in the
extreme, although its name would imply an overhanging cloud of smoke—like that part of Edin-
burgh known as the "Auld *Reekie*"—but only
refers, here, to some hot-water springs in the
neighbourhood, that frequently form clouds of
steam. The town is built upon one end, or corner,
of a great plain, consisting entirely of lava, with
just enough earth to allow some wide patches of
grass upon its surface, and a fair sprinkling of
farmhouses, but, as this part has been inhabited
ever since the Norwegian settlement of Iceland,
the date of this lava and the fact of its being
here at all, would pertain to Iceland in the Pre-
historic Times!

More than a fortnight at Reikjavik was no
unfortunate delay, and I only then weighed
anchor for the north because of a grand opportunity for seeing all the coast, which was

given by the good ship *Jon Sigurdsson.*
Previous to this, many days had been spent, and
excursions made, with the excellent Bishop of
Iceland and his family, or their friends, whose
kindness knew no end. Three or four persons
invariably came in for breakfast with me of a
morning, the table being laid as if for dinner, according to custom, with bottles, glasses, and wine.
Breakfast over, we went out, either sailing on the
bay, or else on a visit to some country house,
where all was merriment—the family, very often,
haymaking as we arrived. Of such a kind was
Bessestadr, the residence of an able and learned
Icelander, Grimr Thomsson. At this house we
were waited on by a good-looking servant girl,
dressed in the complete Icelandic costume, which
for the day-time has nothing remarkable if we
except a small head-covering always black, with
a tassel fastened on by silver and thrown over the
shoulder at one side. We had some tea here in
the evening that resembled cowslip, but stronger,

and which grew, according to Thomsson, in the country. On my endeavouring to find out whereabouts it grew, and under what name, all he would say was, " The women make it; they know all about it; I am not troubled with those things."

Another place visited was Ellidavatn, where lived a man of entirely opposite political opinions, but of great ability, Benedict Sveinsson, who now holds a post of great responsibility under the government of Denmark. Here we had some wild duck shooting, on a lake in front of the house, and used his boat. This gentleman made me the *diplomatic* present of an ivory snuff box ornamented with silver, made out of the tusk of a walrus, which kind of ivory is rarely, if ever, cut into any shape. On his estate (the land only pasture or preserved for hay) was a first-rate salmon river, but I saw no fishing in the proper way, although salmon are taken in great quantity with nets during July and August, especially in the east of Iceland, more delicate in flavour than elsewhere, but hardly ever weighing more than 20lb.

Of excursions by water, sailing was the order ‘of the day, and different islands in the Faxa Fjord were made the object; such as Videy, the seat of a very old family named Stephensson, containing the ruins of a monastery, and a printing press, used only at the Reformation. The mansion itself, built of stone, bore evident marks of decay on the outside, but, inside, had an elaborate cornice round the ceiling; while upon the walls were various portraits in chalk, of the different members of the family, one of whom had been Governor of Iceland, of whose three sons, one became President of the Supreme Court of Justice, also a councillor of state, the next became Governor of the Western district, and the third son, secretary to the Court of Justice. The present man treated us to coffee, the invariable custom on arriving at a house, and overhauled for our benefit a quantity of old silver of very curious workmanship; chains, clasps, rings, buckles, and belts, inherited from generation to generation; but the only kind of *plate* I ever saw in Iceland,* was the so-called Apostle Spoon, preserved in some families to the number of a whole set, but very hard to purchase now; also a tankard on the bishop's dinner-table, and a tumbler of cut glass one day at dinner with the Governor, which would have to go—as he told me while I sat next him—to his successor.

Engey, another island, was made the object of a separate voyage; here was a farmhouse, with eider ducks, undomesticated, building and laying in the yard. No guns are allowed to be fired during the breeding season of these eider ducks, either upon the islands, or within a certain distance of the coast, so great is the esteem in which the people hold this bird, as nearly to remind one of

---

Except some very valuable pieces and of great antiquity, found not unfrequently upon the altars in the churches; forbidden to be sold or to leave the country.

that regard paid in old time to the sacred ibis.
And the eider duck has confidence in man, for a
little boy would lift up the egg when still
warm and replace it, without fear of making her
desert the nest. Three times will the eider duck
spread a lining of its down, and twice is that
lining allowed to be removed, but if taken away
the third time, that nest will be resorted to no
more. This eider down is a great article of commerce with the Icelanders, who sell a pound of it
in weight for eight, and sometimes nine, rix-dalers
(£1). Another great article of trade, especially
in winter time, is the ptarmigan. These birds are
brought down in large quantities by the country
people from all parts and sold to the merchants
of Reikjavik for 2d. or 4d. each, by whom they
are sold again, at Copenhagen, for 6d. or 8d.
apiece, by way of profit.

A third island visited was Andresey, an expedition rendered charming as we sailed home by
some very perfect music from the ladies, and by

a sunset, such as only may be seen upon that amphitheatre of mountains which surround the Faxa Fjord; making this life at Reikjavik resemble that of much more southern climates, peaceful and dreamlike. Boats, laden like waggons with cut hay, would be seen coming slowly into the harbour, especially of a bright summer evening.

There had been a confirmation of young children before visiting this last island, at a church on the way called Brautarholt, which leads me here to mention having witnessed (of ceremonies in the Icelandic church) that of ordination also, at which the bishop wore his vestment of crimson, violet and gold, that had been worn by many more before him, and the newly ordained minister at once entered on his office, by preaching a sermon then and there. All ministers belonging to the church of Iceland wear a white ruff, which will sometimes give a dignified and venerable appearance; and the churches in Iceland number about 280, which, for a scattered population of only 70,000, gives four churches to each thousand people.

The learned and worthy Bishop had taken care to have his family taught music, and well they now repaid him : we used often to go in of an evening, to hear his daughters play or sing.

At dinner one day, when the number was sixteen, while we sat round a square table face to face (only gentlemen) and the ceremony of touching each others' glasses had been performed all round, the conversation turned upon a subject which appears not yet to have died out, though many people in the present day would say it had, or was only superstition : concerning the existence of the Utilegumanna, or race of Outlaws, as to whether any of them still inhabited the country. Nobody would contradict the Bishop, but his lordship was willing to discuss the matter gravely, as the present company consisted of Icelanders (all but the writer), whose imagination, warm as that of Oriental nations, had

peopled the unknown regions of their own land
with a race of other men; and were not to be
shaken so easily in their belief. It was carried in
the end against the Outlaws, and the Utilegumanna
lost the day. But the notion that formerly pre-
vailed, which I give as translated by Magnusson,
was that, "in ancient times, grave crimes were
punished by outlawry; and he upon whom this
sentence was pronounced might choose for
himself either absence from his country, or re-
tirement into its wildest and most difficult
fastnesses, in which latter case he had to support
himself by hunting and fishing, those untrodden
deserts being full of game, and scattered over with
lakes innumerable." Also "the freshness of this
old belief is wonderful. Several places are named
as being the particular haunts of outlaws, and
may show by their names that they have actually
been the resorts of such folk; let us mention, for
instance, the Odadahraun or 'lava of misdeeds.'"
But "they are often men of high and unscrupu-

lous good faith and honour, the which many stories will prove. And when an outlaw has given his promise, or has received some kindness, he will seldom, if ever, prove ungrateful or break his word." The ladies of this family, as in other houses of the richer class, did not sit at table ; but received us after dinner in their drawing-room, when we shook hands according to Icelandic custom, saying the meal was over, and returned them many thanks.

The valuable Library at Reikjavik was also a favourite place of resort, though by far the greater part of its contents were in the old Icelandic tongue, very hard to understand. This language is no branch of any other in the world, but the Swedish, Danish and Norwegian, are different branches of *it*. Spoken by the Norsemen at the time they were invading these very shores in the early part of English history, the originality of this ancient language has continued in Iceland unbroken till now, preserved by their literature

and isolation from the rest of Europe, while the
different branches of it, originally one and the
same, have undergone no end of alteration.   In
Germany the language spoken centuries ago,
from which the present one is taken, came of the
same great family; but the original of this
member is no more, while that from which the
Swedish, Danish and Norwegian are derived has
been preserved in Iceland. Their greatest author,
whose works are still a touchstone whereby all
other writers have been tested and are still compared, is Snorro Storelsson, who lived in the
thirteenth century, and has been called the
" greatest of Icelanders," qualified, however, by his
also being called " the meanest." Celebrated for
poetic talents and great wit, this worthy lived a
great deal at the court of Norway, succeeded to
a very large amount of land belonging to his
family in Iceland, used always to attend the
Althing with a powerful retinue, became soon
popular and won the people's confidence, then

afterwards attempted to destroy their independence and transfer his country to the power of Norway, no doubt hoping it would subsequently make him Iceland's king ; forgetful of the reason his country had been colonised at all—to escape from the dominion of Harold Harfager. The opening sentence of his greatest work, called after the first word in the original ' Heimskringla,' has been translated thus : " It is said that the earth's circle which the human race inhabits is torn across into many bights, so that great seas run into the land from the out-ocean. Thus it is known that a great sea goes in at Niorvasund,* and up to the land of Jerusalem. From the same sea a long sea bight stretches toward the north-east, and is called the Black Sea, and divides the three parts of the earth ; of which the eastern part is called Asia, and the western is called by some Europe, by some Ænea." He professed only to give a chronicle of the kings of

* Straits of Gibraltar.

Norway, but gave a history of all the nations upon earth—so far as it was possible for him to do. Snorro Sturluson (or Storelsson) was murdered, but will always be regarded as the Herodotus of his own land; the language of which is clear, copious, and of great extent, while those who have learnt the same consider it as classical and pure as Greek.

It was in the Icelandic newspaper I first ascertained the recovery of Dr. Livingstone, when found by Mr. Stanley. This newspaper is regularly taken in by one or two of my acquaintances in England, always to be recognized at once by the Icelandic postage stamp on the outside, similar to that of Denmark in appearance at first sight, but easily distinguished by the superscription "Island" (*pronounced Izland.*) Very well worth seeing were the MSS. kindly exhibited at different houses to Gudmundr and me, such as that of Assessor Pjetursson, where we sat and turned over what it was impossible to read, the charac-

ters being scarcely legible even to the owner, so
it was a great relief when coffee was brought in
by daughters of the house, (who also had prepared
it themselves) in a very graceful manner, and in
national costume. The same ceremony was
bestowed upon us at Sigurdsson's, head of the
University here: delicious cream was set before
us by his daughters, with very old and massive
spoons of silver, which would go probably to his
successor in the office—and Dr. Sigurdsson, I
hear with great regret, is there no longer, having
died that very autumn. His elder brother, Jon
Sigurdsson, the greatest of Icelanders now living,
is considered the representative of Icelandic interest at Copenhagen, holding in that city an
important trust. From this college of Reikjavik,
" such as study at the university of Copenhagen
are generally distinguished from their fellow
students by the quickness of their apprehension,
their unwearied application, and their insatiable
thirst for knowledge."

One day there anchored in front of the Icelandic capital, visiting these latitudes, the yacht
Wilja,—rigged as a fore-and-aft schooner, with
standing bowsprit and jib-boom, of 23 feet
beam, and length over all 149 feet, on deck 137
feet; tonnage 366. I heard she was a fine sailing
schooner, and her steam was but 40 horse power
(only auxiliary), but would drive her at a speed of
9 knots in smooth water. She belonged to His
Serene Highness the Prince de Sayn-Wittgenstein of Russia, was built at Gosport, and had
her interior fitted up with every indication of
Moscovian magnificence and taste. Beside the
prince himself, Pierre Dominique Louis, was a
younger brother and one of his cousins, the three
on a voyage round the world. They were accompanied by a scientific man to make observations
upon the geology, botany, and natural history
of every country they might visit, with sketches;
also by a musician, who kept the diary, but
whose only regular employment was to play the

piano whenever they might call for it, in the principal saloon. The whole ship's company were Finlanders: and of all the tribes in the Russian empire these make, it is said, the best sailors, being at the same time very orderly on shore. While here, his serene highness did me the honour of calling one afternoon, and came with the Governor of Iceland at a moment when I happened to be in. Not knowing French half so well as the prince, and being at that time in the way of speaking Danish only, which the prince did not a word, the Governor became our interpreter; so whatever the prince said was in French to the interpreter to be put into Danish for me, and whatever I had to say was in Danish to the interpreter to be put into French for the prince. So it went on, whereas if I had spoken Russian, or the prince had known some English, there would not have been all this to and fro translation of Danish into French, or French, by the same token, into Danish. Here was a vestige

of the Tower of Babel, a wave still undulating
after that unfortunate dispersion—of our race!

Sunday, August 11*th.*—Weighed anchor for
the north of Iceland, for a voyage round the
coast, in the screw steamboat *Jon Sigurdsson* of
Bergen. Between Norway and Iceland there is
considerable trade. A company this year had
started the above steamship to ply between
Bergen and the different ports of Iceland, also
to carry passengers. This evening, Sunday, a
great number from Reikjavik went on board, in
order to visit friends and acquaintances up the
country, preferring the journey by sea. Myself
excepted, the whole company were Icelanders,
both ladies and gentlemen ; so many, in fact, left
Reikjavik, that a worthy citizen who remained
behind saw fit to remonstrate by saying, " Leave
some one, my lord—leave us a few here."

Taking Gudmundr, with Geir Zöega our guide
as before, we got under way, and scarcely a
ripple was visible upon the sea as we crossed the

open bay of Faxa Fjord, and the stars coming
out in due time (arctic twilight so late in the
season being nearly over) made it a beautiful
evening. Every one remained on deck, some
enlivened it by a few songs—and whatever have
been written in Icelandic appear likely to outlive
the light and fugitive pieces in Swedish or Danish
that, with some exceptions, have been composed
to suit the fashion of the day. As a specimen,
however, of the Swedish language, and of the
songs that were sung on this beautiful evening,
I shall give the words of that national song of
Finland, alluded to before:—

> Hör, hur herlig sången skallar
> Mellan Wainös runshaller
> 　Det är Suomis sång
> Hör, de höga furor susa
> Hör, de djupa strömmar brusa,
> 　Det är Suomis sång!

> Se, bland drifvor högt vid polen
> Strålar klar midsommar-solen
> 　Det är Suomis sång:
> Se! på himlens mörka båga
> Nattens norrskern flammar låga
> 　Det är Suomis sång!

Och de väna, blyga dalar
Der en bäck bland blomstren talar :
  Det är Suomis sång.
Och de skogbekrönta fjellar
Lekande i stjerne-qväller—
  Det är Suomis sång.

Öfver allt en röst oss bjuder
Öfver allt en stämma bjuder :
  Det är Suomis sång.
Broder ! eger du ett hjerta
I dess tjusning, i dess smärta
  Hör blott Suomis sång !

In the morning "oh, so early!" we all awoke
by hearing a steady, long-continued whistle, on
the steamboat's part, which gave notice to the
inhabitants of a small station here upon the
north side of the bay that she had arrived. The
captain said to me, "These fellows don't seem to
understand a steamboat; look at the only small
boat they have put out, coming alongside here as
if it wanted to harpoon a whale." The appearance
of this coast, for miles upon the north side and
outside corner of this bay, was something extraordinary; basaltic columns like we have at the

Giant's Causeway and the Isle of Staffa, of
various shapes and sizes, some even standing in
the sea. It is probable that the waters of the
sea, according to a native Icelander and man
of science, Eggert Olafsson, obtained access to
the lava while yet in a heated state ; but no
eruptions have taken place in any part of the
surrounding country since the island first became
inhabited—not therefore since the memory of
man. Sir George Mackenzie, travelling by land
upon this portion of the coast, thus describes it:
" The coast in the neighbourhood of Stappen is
very remarkable, presenting, for the extent of
about two miles, striking and beautiful columnar
appearances, both in the cliffs which form the
shore, and in the numerous insulated rocks which
appear at different distances from the land. The
ranges of columns, which in general are about
fifty feet high, and perfectly regular in their forms,
are variously broken, in consequence of their
exposure to the action of the sea. In some

places, large caves have been formed, and in two
of these the light is admitted by fissures in the
roof, producing a very singular and striking
effect." To increase the splendour of this
present view, the sun rose, lighting up that
great snow-covered glacier, Snaefell's Yokul, now
sharp and clear against the sky and close at
hand. "Vides ut alta stet nive candidum Soracte!"
Rising directly from the sea this remarkable
mountain appears to be of greater height than
if it were inland. But although merely 4500
feet it has never been ascended by any human
being, foreigner or native, to the highest point;
notwithstanding that "Mackenzie's party, with
whom was the late Sir Henry Holland, attempted
it at the beginning of the century." As we
doubled the promontory where it stood the
compass became nearly useless, so great was the
deviation, owing to the quantity of iron concealed, it was said, in the bosom of this mountain.
There being, however, not the slightest fog we

fetched the other side in course of time and
opened the great bay of Breidi Fjord, making
straight for the important station of Stykkisholm,
without stopping at Olafsvik or meeting any
obstacle to prevent us arriving at the former
village by midday. It is singularly situated,
close to the sea, with cliffs rising sheer out of
the water on different islands in front, as well as
on the mainland either side.

All were received on shore by one Arni
Thorlacius, a great curiosity in his way, and
reputed the richest man in Iceland. His name
had been made known to me in England as a
kind of old Udaller, and I had a high opinion of
him beforehand. On being introduced, moreover,
I found him to be exactly the reverse, and a man
very hard to describe: one who bore a reputation
for great hospitality, but now seemed a total
stranger to the practice of it; a man of hospitality proverbial, but *not practical;* possessing
accomplishments and powers of mind superior

to most men, but unable to show the same in
conversation, manner, or by any outward act; of
parts, but incapable of allowing them ever to be
seen. I called upon him, presented, contrary to
my usual custom, two *letters of introduction*, and
he informed me that there happened in this place
to be an inn for strangers. The guide Geir Zöega
went to that same inn, where I would have sent
him anyhow, he all the while taking very much
to heart not only the habits of the fishermen and
sailors there, but also the behaviour of Arni
Thorlacius; may his being the exception to
Icelandic wit and courtesy—prove the rule.

The governor of Western Iceland, whose
residence was here, sent a young relative to
express his desire to be of use to me in very
cordial terms. "Hospitality is a virtue peculiar
to man, and the obligation is as great to receive
as to **confer.**" **Having** obtained leave to bring
Gudmundr, **we** walked up **to** the government
house, and were **received** at the door by the

excellent Amtmand (as a provincial governor is
always called), who conducted us into the largest
wooden house I had seen, larger than **any** house
in Reikjavik **save** those built of stone, **and bade us**
be seated on **the sofa;** there was no carpet on
the floor **whatever, but** boards well polished, and
the whole interior of his residence very well done
up. After some **time spent in conversation on**
the affairs of Iceland, as to the approaching
change in its constitution, policy **of** Denmark,
&c., dinner was announced, and, **as** there **are no**
menservants in Iceland, an elderly female attended
at the table—who turned **out afterwards to be his**
sister. The governor was himself **a** comparatively young man, and has since **married (I was**
very glad to **hear) one** of the bishop's daughters,
of Reikjavik. **Toasts were** given when the meal
was over, wine **was** taken, and **circled freely.**
There is a certain **class of** gentlemen in Iceland,
now reduced to a few only, **and those** aged ; **they**
are Icelandic gentlemen of **the** old school, **not to**

be surpassed in politeness at any court; of such a kind was old Etatsraad (councillor of state) Jonasson, whom I had the pleasure to meet in Reikjavik, and of him this worthy Amtmand of the west reminded me in some things, more than once.

As the steamboat began to threaten, by whistling and tolling a bell, I now had to make off, but not without this Amtmand (deputy-governor of the west), expressing a wish that we might meet again. That night the ship anchored at Flatey, one of those rocky islands by which this bay is completely studded, some containing vast numbers of eider ducks. Upon one of these islands there lived in anchoritic seclusion a venerable and learned minister, by name Eggers, to visit whom in his library, which was said to be valuable and curious, a celebrated professor at the university of Munich once made a journey to Iceland, for that purpose alone. This island, however, where we came to

anchor now, did for all the rest, and here also
there lived a literary man, by name Gisle
Konradsson, upwards of eighty years of age.
Unable to work out of doors, the remainder of
this good man's life was being passed upstairs, in
a miserable garret, apparently without a living
but what could be earned by copying Icelandic
books of modern date into the ancient character.
I have now, among other MSS., one copied by
him for a consideration from the *ancient* into the
modern character, that legendary poem called
'Eyrikssaga' (or, the story of Eric the Red and
his sons), which describes a very remarkable fact,
the discovery of America in the tenth century by
people from this coast. It was no doubt the
driftwood which led to the discovery of America,
by Iceland, long before the time of Christopher
Columbus. For the coast of North America
was known to Icelandic seamen over 500 years
before his time, and a settlement was made upon
the site which is occupied by Massachusetts now.

In New York the other day a statue was to be
erected, and has probably by this time been
completed, of the original discoverer who set
sail in 983 from one of these very islands, Eric
the Red. Emigration to America from Iceland
now is to the extent of three or four hundred
yearly, and on the increase.

The laws respecting driftwood in Iceland make
it all belong to the owner of the *foreshore* upon
which it has been cast, whoever is the owner of
the land above, to which the foreshore forms a
brim. Before the Reformation in Iceland, wealthy
landowners who had rights to wrecked property
upon their shore, would frequently bequeath part
of the same, as an act of piety, to the Icelandic
church, and have mass said, by means of this
legacy, for their souls. A man without natural
heirs would leave his whole right of driftwood
for the use and benefit of some one church. But
in many cases the benefit conferred upon one
particular church would be of small value, on

account of its distance from the shore and
expense of being taken up, so the parish minister
would claim a head rent instead, according to
ecclesiastical law upon the island, from the
successor to the farm attached.   But the advan-
tages arising from this produce of the sea
compensate in some measure for the total want
of forest in the country, and are fully appreciated
by the Icelanders; so that many places on the
coast sell high, and may be held in possession or
rented by persons living on the opposite side of
the island. Formerly a certain share of this
produce was given to the king (of Denmark
since, but of Norway previously), only that
custom is now entirely at an end. The other
day a difficulty rose in "Jetsam, Flotsam, &
Ligan" upon the coast of Yorkshire, and had to
be decided by the laws of Iceland, because our
own law was unable to do it. On one district of
the coast, very inaccessible and unprotected,
called Horn Strand (near Cape Horn upon the

north), a great quantity of drift timber very
frequently comes in; and it was told me as a
piece of private information (therefore I can only
impart it now in confidence, hoping the reader will
not tell any one), that a merchant of Reikjavik,
once upon a time having fitted out a smack and
made believe it was for fishing, found a whole
accumulation of driftwood upon that very strand
(where, in fact, he went on purpose), sold the same
right and left without losing time or making any
trouble about it, for a very considerable sum, and
then (without leaving any address where to send to
him if necessary) set sail, every *stitch* of canvas!

We left Flatey in fine weather, about mid-day
following, and struck out once more for the open
sea.   Our course lay round the north-west peninsula, that part of Iceland on the map which re-
sembles the Morea in shape and size, the " Mul-
berry leaf" of Iceland, however, being somewhat
larger.   Of Iceland in general, the inhabitants of the
present day are not a hardy race, but very delicate ;

the intermixture by marriage for centuries past of
the same families has weakened their bodily constitution and destroyed their energy : but on this
peninsula they are still the same robust and enter-
prising race that in former time once " ruled the
stormy sea." Very little connection appears to
exist between these natives and the rest, nearly
all the passengers from Reikjavik by this time
having left the ship. And her course began to
lie due north, passing by Latrabjerg Roost, a promontory where two seas appear to meet and
make a very strong current with considerable swell,
though I did not see the necessity of such heaving,
pitching, rolling, and tossing, as the ship gave way
to now. We kept out to sea all night, and, as
early as possible next morning, entered Dyra Fjord,
one of those deep and mysterious gulfs, or narrow
bays, on this peninsula, between immense battle-
ments of perpendicular rock. Lofty and craggy
mountains are here piled one above the other, so
as to be magnificent, surpassing anything I had

previously **seen.** **What** should **we** surprise in here, at anchor, **but the** *Wilja*—showing **the** Russians must be susceptible **of scenery, to come out for it all this way.** Prince de Sayn-Wittgenstein had **told** me himself this would be probably **their next** place **of** resort, but the name not being **at that time familiar, had** entirely escaped my recollection. Business **at a solitary trading** station **here** did **not keep us any** length **of** time, and soon again, in full steam, **our ship** might have been seen—gliding between panoramas of desolation—for some hours. **After she came** out, and had been only a **short time in the** open sea, business compelled her to steam **into** another fjord, this time a great deal wider, and on a stretch **of sand about half** way up, shaped something **like a sickle—whence its** name, Skutilsfjordr— **there** stood before us the **second town of Iceland.**

The **population** of this village is somewhere about three hundred, its exports chiefly salt fish —to Spain, and the markets **on** the Mediterranean,

for the use of the Catholics during Lent--cod
and ling, from £16 to £20 (English equivalent)
per ton, tallow and hides, with a vast amount of
fish-oil, called Tran, worth nearly £60 per ton.
The principal exports of Iceland, however, taking
it all round, are eider down and sheep's wool—
superior to that of Shetland.   Here there are two
inns, one of which has a very fair billiard table.
I took wine at four different houses, so glad the
people were to see a stranger, and then had tea
in the house of a well-to-do merchant, which had
flowers growing in the window, and a piano, going
pretty nearly the whole time.   Here, I believe
the only place in the whole country, they drive
sledges in winter-time, each family keeping its
own.   Gudmundr climbed the rocks to look
for botanical specimens, and met a number of
country people, who had seen the steamer from
the mountains long before she came in, troop-
ing down to exchange their produce for whatever
luxuries she might have on board.

We left Isa Fjord (the name of this bay) in
the evening, and presently came out upon the
open sea. Somewhere about midnight our course
began to lie due east, as we rounded Cape Horn,
opening that ample and far-reaching bay which
runs into the eastern side of this north-west
peninsula, called Huna Flöi.

" *Thursday, Aug.* 15 (private journal).—I am
now within the Arctic circle. No ice whatever.
Hope to see some by-and-by." This was at
midnight, but, had it been day, we might have
seen some part of that great glacier inland, called
Dranga Yokul, which rises about the centre of
that branch of the peninsula we are now passing.
At this time there were very few passengers indeed,
and only Icelanders, who now sat round the cabin
fire. As we talked of the best-looking people,
and where they were to be found—girls, of course
—it was decided, determined, agreed on, and
otherwise laid down, that the best were to be
seen at Akureyri, a village on the north coast, but

a great deal farther eastward, and among the scattered population of the Eyja Fjord, where Akureyri stands !

In the afternoon of the day following, we made the farthest limit of the bay, and came to anchor at Bordeyri. Tired of seeing nothing but the coast, I gave orders to pack up and disembark, leaving the ship to continue between these little trading stations its own desultory way. *Once more let us plunge into the country, live among the people, live their life, and forget all other customs in their own.* I went up to the merchant's house at this station, and was struck by its resemblance to an architectural design in Dasent's translation of an Icelandic Saga, a design representing the old Icelandic Skali, or ancient " hall," and although made of wood, comparatively new, it had, no doubt, been built on the old plan. At this house there was a bust of Jon Sigurdsson, the Icelandic patriot. Gudmundr, not seeming to recognize the likeness, said to me, *ipsissimis in verbis*, " Of whom will this statue be ? "   I quote this to show what sort of English the Icelanders learn to speak.   Latin, compared to what it has been, is not spoken half so generally now—I only remember hearing it on one occasion.   I sat up very late that night over whisky and water, hot, with the merchant, who enlightened me on various points, saying that in his neighbourhood there were *mounds of earth* to mark where formerly had stood the booths of merchants from Ireland, Irishmen, six hundred years ago, so that we had a great deal in common.   More especially as the writer's ancestor, William Canning of Bristol (who had nothing whatever to do with Ireland, but was, nevertheless, a merchant), had a ship trading in Iceland, about the very time when *Christopher Columbus* came, who sailed here from Bristol, to find out everything possible about America, *after* the date of a treaty with Denmark, by which all English ships were prohibited trading here, except those of William Canning, in consideration of a large debt owing to him by that country, and in the Church of St. Mary de Redcliffe may be seen this day, upon his tomb, the list of his ships, one of which is stated there to be "in Iselond" about that very time! *"I called the New World into existence, to redress the balance of the old."*

The polar bear is only a visitor upon the shores of Iceland, floating here in winter time upon the broken ice. About him there is the following superstition, that he is all the while a human being, and born so, but compelled by a curse to appear in this form, which he does not take, however, till the old she bear has laid her *paw* upon him, and if found, or taken away from her, before this can be done, will grow up like any ordinary human being, only troubled with an overwhelming fancy for the sea. A man upon the island of Grimsey, to the north of Iceland, once succeeded in capturing a young specimen—a girl —who became in time one of great and remarkable beauty; but one day, when he was not looking out, she escaped and plunged into the sea, to return to him no more. This belief, however, does not reconcile the Icelanders to the visits of the polar bear; I did not see one the whole time, but have reason to believe that, if ever one were to appear upon the coast, he or she would have a warm reception, and be killed upon the spot.

That night we retired very late, and in the morning made all preparation, by getting horses, packing baggage, trying tent and so on, for a dash into the heart of the country. We had also to take a supply of horse-shoes, for, however expert every Icelander may be in shoeing a horse, high and low, rich and poor, no shoes are to be had upon the way. This department was left entirely to Geir Zöega, who, however, came to me, and said he could not raise horses in the neighbourhood enough, so taking what he had already, I sent him into the *next* neighbourhood for more, and went with Gudmundr to spend that

day with Olaf Palsson, one whose preferment in
the Icelandic church would be equivalent to
rural dean. I found in him not only the kind,
hospitable, and unassuming Icelander, but the con-
sistent and enlightened Christian. Speaking pure
English, this holy man invited us to dine with him,
and made his sons, meantime, play every Icelandic
tune I wished for, on an harmonium which had
been the present of his parish, and taken to him
on a wheelbarrow, which met a sailing-vessel in a
creek near by, where it had put in for the
purpose! Returning that night, I was accompanied by two sons of my host, in fulfilment of a
very ancient custom of the Icelanders, that has
come down from generation to generation, upon
their horses for exactly half the way; when they
dismounted, raised their hats, I raised mine, we
heartily shook hands, and thus behaved like Icelanders of old. Here, in the northern division of
Iceland, the tendency of the people is to rebellion,
more or less, against Denmark; the race is more

independent, their houses are more comfortable and larger, even the horses attain a greater size. This was a common subject of chaff between me and Gudmundr—the inferiority of the south—he never having seen the north before.

On the following morning twelve horses might have been seen wending their uncertain way across one corner of that mighty desert occupying the interior of Iceland, called " Obygd," which means *unbuilt*. Here, for once, the weather failed us; sheets of pouring rain obliterated all the view, until, going down a steep incline between black cliffs all seamed with narrow waterfalls, we entered the ravine of Haugadalr. Thunderstorms in the north of Iceland are unknown; the electricity in the atmosphere of this volcanic region of the earth is worked off in other ways; such a thing as a thunderstorm has happened in the south but very rarely, in the north not since the memory of man. Our way now leading into

this ravine, which became a great deal **wider by-
and-by**, one could **not avoid being struck by**
the appearance **of seclusion** and air **of great**
antiquity about some **farmhouses here and there,**
built with **a simplicity that one would imagine**
might also have been seen before the Flood, or
earlier still, before **mankind** knew **how to build
a city.** The heavy **fall of** rain appeared now to
be spent, and that mist which had surrounded us
upon the upper ground **or** mountain district
of our earlier journey, now disappeared and left
this valley. So simple and yet civilized **is the life**
of this people that one **is** constantly reminded of
the patriarchs of **old.** Nothing have **they for**
riches but their flocks and herds, no corn or
possibility of **failure** in their crops, no fear of
famine ; and always appear to be gratified by
one's visit, however **wet,** travel-stained, **or be-**
clapered **with** mud **one** may arrive. Passing
by several farmhouses, my **caravan halted for the**
night at **one** by name **Leikskali,** where the

ordinary salutation, " Verid Der sælir og blessir,"
I wish thee happiness, or prosperity (same as in
Arabic, " Salam aleik," *All hail !*), having been
exchanged, we gathered round their fire, put on
dry clothes, and heartily enjoyed some supper, all
sitting down to the same board ; " Ceremony was
not invited to the feast, and Nature presided over
the entertainment." Not all the morality from
Confucius down to Addison could make these
people better than they are ! The life in winter-
time here, also, is said to be cheerful enough ; but
different of necessity to any other life upon the
globe, so that any one who wanted to try a new
phase of existence would only need to spend the
winter on this part of our planet, so unlike the
other surfaces of this Earth. I had a great mind
to stay on. It has been thus described by
Dr. Henderson, who spent it in the south of
Iceland, somewhere near Reikjavik : " A winter
evening in an Icelandic family presents a scene
in the highest degree interesting and pleasing.

Between three and four o'clock P.M. the lamp
is hung up in the *bathstofa* or principal apartment, which answers the double purpose of a
bedchamber and sitting room, and all the
members of the family take their station, with
their work in their hands, on their respective
seats, all of which face each other. . . . Besides
preparing the food the females employ their
time in spinning, which is most commonly done
with the spindle and distaff, knitting stockings,
mittens, shirts, &c., as also in embroidering bed-
covers, saddle-cloths, and cushions, which they
execute with much taste, interspersing flowers
and figures of various colours. . . . The work
is no sooner begun than one of the family,
selected on purpose, advances to a seat near the
lamp and commences the evening lecture, which
generally consists of some old Saga, or other
such histories as are to be obtained on the island.
Being but badly supplied with printed books,
the Icelanders are under the necessity of copying

such as they can get the loan of, which sufficiently accounts for the fact, that most of them
write a hand equal in beauty to that of the ablest
writing masters in other parts of Europe. . . .
The custom just described appears to have
existed among the Scandinavians from time immemorial. The person chosen as reciter was (and
is still) called Thulr, and was always celebrated
for his knowledge of past events, and the dignity
and pathos with which he related them." The
same writer describes also : " Every summer, the
people live several weeks on the mountains, in
their tents, which resemble pretty much those of
the Bedoween Arabs, while they are collecting
the Icelandic moss, and are extremely fond of
this kind of nomadic life. The care of the cows
and sheep is left to the female part of the family,
who make curds, butter, cheese, &c., and they
repair in companies about the middle of summer
to collect the Fjallagrös or Iceland moss, in the
uninhabited parts of the country. They have

generally a man or two with them, and the few weeks they spend in this employment in the desert are regarded as the happiest of the whole year. They live in tents, which they remove from place to place, according to the greater or less abundance of the moss." In another passage, "Habituated from the earliest years to hear of the character of their ancestors, and the asylum which their native island afforded to the sciences when the rest of Europe was immersed in ignorance and barbarism, the Icelanders naturally possess a high degree of national feeling, and there is a certain dignity and boldness of carriage observable in numbers of the peasants, which at once indicates a strong sense of independence and propriety."

I am now at Leikskali, in the valley of Haugadalr, and to-morrow, if my horses please, shall be again at Stykkisholm. They tell me it will be fair weather, and I believe it, because I wish it. When the day broke, and we had slept for a considerable time, breakfast was provided, consisting of *skyr*—a dish of coagulated milk, resembling curds in Scotland, only sour; to which is added plenty of sweet milk or cream, and sometimes a peculiar flavour by also adding the juice of various berries, but especially the juniper, a shrub that is by no means scarce in Iceland. The day began tolerably fair, and our caravan took it pretty easily, so I had leisure to make observations on a wild curlew that followed us above, screeching and hovering in a circle for half the day over our heads.

After riding for some hours it became necessary to part with every single horse, give up travelling by land, and take henceforward to the water—for at length we had come to the seashore, and it was agreed beforehand that these horses should be sent back, so as to reach their owners in four days from setting out. Commissioning a man to undertake the same, we now embarked with baggage in a sailing boat

so as to reach Stykkisholm by water. No
sooner had the sail been set, than my men
removed their hats, looked down and appeared
to be engaged in prayer; which is, in fact, a
custom that has always been observed in Iceland
right round the whole sea-coast. This touching
evidence of Christianity in so remote a corner
of the globe, may possibly account for Iceland
having been preserved so many hundred years,
its people being still the same, still in possession
of the land. Another evidence of religion rarely
met with is that " when the Icelander awakes, he
does not salute any person that may have slept
in the room with him, but hastens to the door,
and lifting up his eyes towards heaven, adores
Him who made the heavens and the earth, the
Author and Preserver of his being. He then
returns into the house and salutes every one he
meets, with 'God grant you a good day.'"

Presently we fell in with a strong current,
which swung the boat right round one island and

between two more, this being a particular passage that is only made use of to gain time, and called " the Irish way," *Irska leid,* because in olden times some Irish merchants had a trading station also on this coast.   There is a " fjord" or narrow bay in the north-west peninsula, called *Patriks* Fjord ; but we are now entering the Breidi Fjord, and approaching Stykkisholm in a direction opposite to where the steamer had come in before. Arrived on shore, we were welcomed once more by the deputy-governor, who this time invited us to stay the night, and showed the way upstairs to a spacious bedroom, in which my bed was made with mattresses of eider down, pure and simple. The sensations on sinking into this have been admirably described by Sir George Mackenzie : "To a stranger, crawling under a huge feather bed seems *rather alarming.* But, though very bulky, the down of the eider duck is very light, and a bed which swells to the *thickness of two or three feet* weighs no more than four or five

pounds.   At first, the sensations produced by this
light covering were very agreeable ; but the
down being one of the very worst conductors of
heat, the accumulation soon became oppressive ;
and at length we were under the necessity of *getting
rid* of the upper bed, to escape the proofs of the
good qualities of eider down, which we now
experienced to an intolerable degree."

As we were in no particular hurry to leave the
excellent Amtmand or his comfortable house,
and had also to raise a fresh supply of horses, I
did not get under way till twelve o'clock,
which, considering a ride of nine hours lay before
us, was late enough. The sun shone with a
brilliant intensity that made these volcanic,
charred mountains all sparkle not unlike some
costly mineral, exceeding in beauty of this
character all that I had seen before ; I say these
mountains, for we are now entering the same
region the steamer had coasted with me the first
day, and *to-night !* I shall sleep at the foot of

Snaefells Yokul, the great glacier. Meantime, the new cavalcade is winding among mountains of extraordinary shape; some like gigantic dust heaps of black sand, wind-swept and rounded on the summit to a point. I have seen, but elsewhere in Iceland, craters of moderate height scattered over a volcanic plain, precisely similar, by astronomical discovery, to the scenery upon the Moon. The view here was grand indeed, but awful, riveting the admiration. I cantered on, to look at it alone. Beholding it on every side of deadly black and silent as the grave, without one sign of life or vegetation, I felt like one who has wandered into the 'Inferno' of Dante. I understood the old tradition, that Satan had been the creator of this gloomy region of the earth, and saw how there " still lingered majesty" upon the work, of the Fallen Angel. Milton's 'Paradise Lost,' in which that Evil One appears to be the hero, has been very well translated into Icelandic; of which translation it is said "that the entire poem never having been printed is a real loss to Scandinavian literature: as it not only rises superior to any other translation of Milton, but rivals, and in many instances in which the Eddaic phraseology is introduced, seems almost to surpass the original itself."

However that may be, I was glad when the rest of the party came up, when our caravan descended by a rocky gorge into a valley, which presently spread out and disclosed views of a more earthly character, in the shape of lakes and plains. Passing by a crag upon the left, there sat a pair of eagles, a male and female of the golden eagle, which never moved until we were so close I scarcely could believe them to be wild; in Iceland they are never shot, and the eagle in consequence of this appears to have lost its fear of man. After this, we opened a considerable lake upon the right some way below, and saw with a field glass a couple of wild swans, also their cygnets. Swans abound in Iceland, but never more than two live on the same piece of water *inland*, until the season for their young is over; but Iceland is scattered over with lakes innumerable, often in the mountains, generally on the border of some plain. And in such lakes there is an Ossianic mystery, a wild sweetness. Often have I stopped in heartfelt wonder at the soft and subduing influence of some dark, silver, solitary lake, and turned the horse's head to go back to it without taking off my gaze. Nothing but forest is wanted to place this among the most wonderfully beautiful countries upon earth; and were it not for the uncleanliness of the poorer population, I might possibly agree with the poet William Morris (author of 'Jason,' 'Defence of Queen Guinevere,' &c.) in describing Iceland as part of his 'Earthly Paradise.' Overhead, as in Switzerland, there may be snow-covered mountains in some parts, and glaciers, such as the celebrated Snaefells Yokul

we are coming **to, or the widely** remote Dranga
Yokul, or that magnificent and **long-way-visible**
ice mass called Eyriks **Yokul, in the heart of the**
Icelandic desert. During **the winter the whole**
interior of Iceland, within a very short distance of
the sea, is buried more **or** less **by snow, like the**
"winding sheet of a dead land." **But** this only
makes it by so much the more fertile in summer,
like Egypt after the inundation of the Nile, **and**
the cows, feeding **on the richest,** sweetest **grass,**
yield milk and cream far better **than I found in**
Switzerland; moreover, we **have now entered**
Snaefells Syssel, **the very "county" of all Iceland**
for variety of produce, natural history, **miner-**
alogy, or sea shells upon **the** coast **;** receiving on
both sides the benefit of **the Gulf Stream, as it is**
surrounded very **nearly** by the sea.

Continuing **our way** between **mountains of**
great height, we met another caravan, consisting of **a wealthy Icelandic merchant and his**
party, **with whom,** after profound salutation, I

drank some first-rate Muscatelle, from a cup of silver. We had each dismounted, and my new acquaintance requested I would honour him by receiving the keys of his larder and cellar, which this genuine Icelander handed to my guide ! We were going, anyhow, to visit him, and only separated, promising to meet on his return.

Soon after this appeared before us a bit of Faxa Fjord, and at dusk our road lay for some hours along the margin of its coast ; and we did not arrive till very late that night at the house of this generous man, Gudmundsson, one of the trading stations of Iceland, called Budir, built of brick from Copenhagen, with, on one side, a large wooden store house, depôt of the whole surrounding country. That evening I was deeply impressed by a piece of Icelandic behaviour on the part of an old man : hearing somehow that Gudmundr was in the place, this aged Icelander came into our parlour, asked him one or two questions in Icelandic, then raised the young

fellow's hand with tenderness and pressed it to his
lips. It appeared that my companion's mother
had spent her childhood in this neighbourhood,
and been a favourite of this man in his youth;
that forty years or so had passed away, but made
no difference in *his* feelings; and the sentiments,
which had been concealed in his life all this time,
now found their expression towards her son.
Perhaps I ought not to have been there.

Having now arrived at the very foot of
Snaefells Yokul, on the west coast of the island,
between Faxa Fjord and Breidi Fjord, I fell that
night into a profound slumber; and on awaking
the day after, saw this glorious mountain from
the window, rising within easy reach. It was a
fine morning; and

> " You could not see a cloud, because—no cloud was in the
> sky."

but never till to-day having attempted any
glacier work, various causes of delay prevented
me from starting until noon, the Icelanders

hoping secretly that some cause or other would prevent it after all "as an act of presumptuous temerity. They regard the mountain with a kind of superstitious veneration; and find it difficult to divest their minds of the idea that it is still haunted by Barda, the tutelary divinity of the glacier, who will not fail to avenge himself on all that have the audacity to defile, with mortal breath, the pure and ethereal atmosphere of his abode." The guide, Geir Zöega, declaring that he was not equal to it, I made him find some other man who was, and a rope, with a couple of iron headed poles (which these people actually had, but very primitive), and to put up whatever we might want to eat in case of not returning home that night. Leaving Gudmundr to take care of his old man, I began the expedition, to his great disappointment—for he was all eagerness to go—with only one young Icelander, very little older than himself. This gentleman had been upon the glacier (at least he said so) once before, and had a trowel, which he intended to use like an ice axe, for cutting steps. We started on horseback. At first there was a ride of two hours, the inhabitants of different farm-houses each staring, as they always will, at any one who tries a mountain expedition: no doubt wondering if Barda* would forgive the presumption of this undertaking, or find means to protect his seat. At two o'clock P.M. we left our horses in charge of some one; at four, after getting up some way and traversing a whole district of loose pumice stones, *gained the ice.*

We pushed on. Pure and transparent as the atmosphere upon this glacier proverbially is, the deception of it led us on for a considerable time in full view of the summit, before we knew or had any idea how far the summit actually was. But as this annihilation of distance appeared to be somewhat supernatural we did not believe it,

---

* "Antiquum montis hujus incolam dominum Bardum Snae-fellsas, cujus sine auspiciis mons Snaefell Yokul vix ac ne vix quidem superari potest."—*Vidalin.*

and accordingly went straight on; the snow was in good order, and promised an easy ascent.

Yawning fissures in the ice came frequently across the way, sometimes of great width, and compelling us to go right round; very beautiful to look into, but of a frightful depth, and lit up with a blue-green colour. Delighted by every prospect of accomplishing what the good people of Reikjavik had declared impossible, I strove to reach the summit before night. But the guide complaining of some sickness that he felt, and since the evening already had set in, I found it necessary to retrace the way—no easy matter upon ice—and find somewhere to pass the night on *terra firma.*

That night was spent upon the mountain. With a stone and a piece of waterproof upon it for our pillow, this man and I slept in the open air. At daybreak, half past two, we set to work again—by the light of a splendid sunrise, Oriental in beauty and grandeur. None of the

vapour of England rose here to prevent our view
of two seas (Breidi Fjord and Faxa Fjord) at
once ; while the low coasts and harbours around
each, lay spread out underneath us like a map.
It has been said, that from some one part of the
great channel which lies between Iceland and
Greenland, Snaefells Yokul may be seen on
one side, and another lofty mountain in Greenland, upon the other. We are now, or would be
if upon the top, looking out towards Greenland,
due west, but distant about 250 miles. At first
the ice and snow work was a pretty piece of
business, for it had all frozen over since last
evening and afforded scarcely any footing whatever, so, until the rising sun had somewhat
thawed the surface, we were hardly able to make
any head. However, by cutting a step here and
there we overcame the slopes of ice ; and by
seven o'clock or somewhat about that time, in
four hours after commencing the ice work,
arrived within only a quarter of the highest

point.   But all this while my unfortunate and
inefficient guide had been making signs apparently as if he felt some kind of illness coming
on, more by his manner than by any positive
communication, and at last sank right down
upon the snow, utterly powerless to proceed
another step, with blood from his ears and in his
eyes! Never in my life having travelled with a
medicine chest, I did not know what on earth to
do with him—could only hold up and support
his head, as he lay helpless on the crisp and
dazzling snow. Here we were, on a lovely
morning, with the whole day before us and not a
cloud in sight, unable to proceed. I tried to
make him eat, thinking the present halt would
be a good opportunity for breakfast, but
nothing was able to restore him—the short
supply of spirits had been wanted for last night;
and there was but a melancholy satisfaction to
the present writer in thus breakfasting alone,
upon a piece of genuine Icelandic mutton,

however delicious that might be—and it was *uncommonly* good upon that frosty morning, in fact it made the summit appear even closer than before! The prize is very nearly in our grasp. But the fellow still lay groaning here upon the snow, and how was I to leave him.

He was evidently unable to breathe atmosphere so rarefied and thin; directly, therefore, it was possible to move him, we descended, having lost the grandest opportunity of doing what, in Iceland, would have made any man, native or foreigner, immortal.

The earlier in the summer this glacier is attempted, the easier it will be ; for the ice has not cracked and split into chasms like we now had to encounter, and the winter snow, still undissolved, remains in one steady slope the whole way up, making allowance for the possibility of places where one might sink in, if the chasms of last year have only been partly drifted over. No sooner had we left the ice, than this unhappy

man became all right, to my considerable satisfaction, and I returned with him to Budir, getting
back quite early in the day, without any result ;
so, having said what will describe this haunted
glacier, and given some faint outlines for the
benefit of travellers to come, I wish the evil
genius who lives upon it—farewell ; and hope the
laurels which I did not win, may fall upon that
man, who, favoured more by Fortune, shall first
succeed in making the ascent.

CHAPTER III.

FROM ICELAND TO NORWAY.

AT length it was time to leave Iceland, which I did with great regret, having lived among the people and become accustomed to their mode of life; and having resisted the invitation of a neighbour of my host to stay with him for a week and get some seal shooting, I rode for three days—on one day thirteen hours in the saddle—to Hvalfjord; and, as this was now three hundred and sixty miles I had travelled in Iceland on horseback, from this point crossed over to Reikjavik by open boat. The steamboat *Jon Sigurdsson* had come back to Reikjavik, after finishing her business in the

north, probably at Akureyri, where I did not
happen to go with her, on account of disem-
barking at Bordeyri on the way. That same
Akureyri is a thriving place, and the only village
on the whole north coast; blocked up with ice,
however, during winter. The steamboat *Jon
Sigurdsson* had come back to Reikjavik, and
was continuing her course that very night across
the Atlantic and German oceans, to Bergen,
in Norway. But she was only, by rights, a river
steamer, not built for open sea at all ; and, having
had doubts about her while upon the passage
round the coast, I would not go with her to
Norway ; did not like one or two things,
and so declined what would appear to be the
shortest and most comfortable route. Wishing
to go on to Norway, I determined to engage a
boat and sail over. This resolution, moreover,
was seconded by the sight of a small sloop in the
harbour, among other ships, one which was of only
six-and-twenty tons. I may here be allowed to

mention that the steamboat *Jon Sigurdsson* was compelled, it was told me afterwards in Norway, to return to Reikjavik for safety upon this very voyage, unable to meet the rough weather and heavy seas; and that, on getting eventually to Bergen, she was sent into dock and never tried this passage any more.   So I engaged the six-and-twenty, making her wait till the day after, the wind promising to be still fair, or anyhow to take us out of Faxa Fjord into the open sea.

"*Sunday, August* 25*th* (private journal).— Farewell to all, with great regret.   This evening, came on board."

It would be difficult to express my feelings on being shown the only small cabin we had to get into, five feet by four, and the only satisfaction was in knowing one would have to lend a hand on board, so live on deck, thus only be at night below or in spare time.   For our whole ship's company consisted of a skipper and three hands, myself extra, together with a man who served out the provisions, took care of everything on board, kept the cabin clean, and so on.

> " Ah! what pleasant visions haunt me
>   As I gaze upon the sea!
> All the old romantic legends,
>   All my dreams come back to me,
> Till my soul is full of longing
>   For the secret of the sea,
> And the heart of the great ocean
>   Sends a thrilling pulse through me."

Early on Monday morning, the 26th of August, before daylight, I heard them weigh the anchor, and very soon became aware we had set sail. Keeping the south coast of Faxa Fjord, with the land upon our left, and open bay upon the right, we set her square-sail and went out to westward with a favourable east wind, but slowly; and did not pass the cape called Reikjanaes till half past eight that evening, about which time we furled her square-sail, no longer having to run before the wind, and brought her round, directly she had left Cape Reikjanaes, to keep close to the wind, our course over to Norway now lying pretty nearly due east. *Ingolf,* our vessel, was cutter-rigged. She had formerly been a fishing smack, full built aft, and was taking now for ballast a cargo of close packed Icelandic wool—at least I was told so, but never saw it. With only one mast, she had a jib, foresail, mainsail, and gaff topsail that we never used; the square-sail, only when she could run before the wind. Her length over all was fifty feet, breadth of beam eighteen feet, speed, with a fair wind, nine knots (which, for her feeble proportions, was not at all bad)—close-hauled, would keep four points up to the wind. And now that we had got her fairly out, presently the wind fell: there was no mistake about it, she was becalmed already. The hands, of whom two have since been drowned, being only fishermen, instantly threw out their lines, but to my profound satisfaction got nothing by it, as I had begun to fear they might neglect our progress, poor fellows, for their favourite pursuit. As we lay to until night they pointed out a huge

and shapeless rock, looming in the distance, of
great height.   Here was the last resort of that
bird, now become extinct, celebrated as the Gair
Fowl, or Great Auk ; extinct, no doubt, like other
birds of history, such as the dodo, the moa, and
many others, of which some are only known by
geological discovery.   Standing some way out to
sea, the spray dashing up to it even in calm
weather, I had a good view of this inaccessible and
dismal omen of many a shipwreck that might be.
Here this extraordinary bird, of the same genus as
the penguin, was at one time so abundant that its
eggs were taken by the boatload, whenever a boat
had access; and now, for the blown shell of one
in the writer's collection £60 was offered the
other day.   If the great auk is existing anywhere
at all, it would only be, and still might be,
on those other islands off the coast of Iceland in
the middle of Breidi Fjord ; but the last that is
known to have been seen was killed in 1845, upon
this precipitous and gloomy rock, Gairfuglasker.

Our skipper was a young Norwegian, 27 years of age; had been to the college of Bergen, and there learnt, or passed a satisfactory examination in, the rudiments of navigation. A village on the coast of Norway, called in Icelandic *Olafssund*, Norwegian *Aalesond*, a little to the south of Christianssund, was the port to which we made. Clad like the ordinary common hand, I wore an oilskin pilot coat, trowsers of the same, a sou'-wester, and fishing-boots that came above the knee; which turned out necessary later on, as the small size of our vessel made the sea wash over heavily.

Nor was it long before there came an opportunity of seeing what our craft could do. For, at midnight, after that very lull, the wind got up and presently blew hard. Had it only been from the west, this would have taken us along, instead of rising from that very quarter to which her course now lay. Towards morning, Tuesday the 27th, this became a gale. No hope remained of making any head; we very soon found we must at once take in all sail, lash the helm, set a mere bit of the mainsail to keep her steady—head a little to the wind—while she drifted, and we had nothing for it but to lay to and let her drive, in the direction of Greenland, miles and miles to leeward, far out of her course. Not often has a vessel of such frail dimensions to live in such a sea. It was a slender outfit. She had made the run before, but only once, and then it was *from* Norway to Iceland at a very different season. All it was now possible for man to do was done, and these fellows behaved well, said nothing, but did their duty. That was no great matter all the same, for when everything was done that skill could do it rested with herself to live or not, while we trusted to her timbers. Whenever there was anything to call us out on deck I used to see frequently the skipper, sometimes a common seaman, frantically wave his hand, as if in great anxiety, endeavouring to warn off some gigantic wave in full swing bearing down upon us, larger than the rest; whether this habit is common to all sailors or peculiar to Norwegians, I did not trouble to ascertain. For sixty hours the sea raged on without abating. On the first day a whole plank in the gunwale was shattered and washed away, to appear again no doubt upon the shores of Iceland as driftwood, while the vessel shook and trembled, seeming likely to be smashed and broken up by any large wave now that might break over her. More of her gunwale was shivered in the night, and not until then did these fishermen throw out a floating anchor, which they contrived, however, to do now, and immediately it appeared to break the violence of the Atlantic, checking at once the fury of these rollers; but not sufficiently, for on the second day towards evening another plank was driven in upon the weather side. This last was patched up somehow, but the other three that wanted looking to were not to be repaired, and so continued in that state for the whole voyage. There was no carpenter on board.

On the third day, Thursday the 29th, at twenty minutes before twelve noon, the rough weather began to give over; but the swells of the Atlantic —we were now far out, and unable to see land— did not go down till evening. On conjecturing we had by this time drifted just a hundred miles to westward, we found by our quadrant at noon on the day after, with the log, that she lay south-west of Cape Reikjanaes exactly, a good eighty miles out of her course. A little more, and the distant coast of Greenland might have come in view.

Friday, 30th.—We made no progress; after the heavy seas came a dead calm; and one might have said of the Atlantic Ocean then, in the words of the ' Ancient Mariner,'

> " So lonely 'twas that God Himself
> Scarce seemed there to be."

That evening, however, about eight P.M. a little

wind rose in the north, and our sails, already spread, began to be filled out. I turned into my narrow berth and slept until eleven the next morning, a berth in the only cabin that we had save a place for'ard where the common hands lived and got into by a ladder; but this was the after cabin and had room for two, so I shared it with the skipper. Our berths were on each side, and comfortable enough once entered, but the struggle was to get in, so famously were they protected against the possibility of rolling out, so alarming, on account of this precaution, was the small size of the entrance! The only furniture of our apartment was a clock upon the wall, and underneath it a plain table; in the only drawer of that table were our charts, calendar, and quadrant. We had no chronometer; nor any telescope whatever in the whole ship, but a *binocular* which I was taking to Norway for the reindeer answered that purpose, and was all that one could wish for, if not more also than was actually wanted, out at sea; we never spoke a ship the whole time.

The following day, Saturday the 31st of August, was bright and the wind moderate, but fair. Private journal: "Still far out in the North Atlantic, though now upon our course, and saw the first sail we have seen since Monday last of any visible description, sort, or kind." The skipper kept his own log of the voyage, so that I had little else to write than what is here:

"*Sunday, Sept. 1st.*—Glorious day. Wind north-west. Saw other sails, and a huge whale also, not far off.

"*Monday, 2nd.*—Wind not so fair, but still enabled us to beat another larger vessel, going the same way. Several whales in sight.

"*Tuesday, 3rd.*—Took my turn as usual of an hour or more at the helm, with leave from skipper, who now left me in sole management.

"*Wednesday, 4th.*—There has risen in the night such a gale from the east as to make our feeble fishing smack, for such it is, roll like a reel. Took two and a-half hours at the tiller.

" *Thursday, 5th.*—Same wind, same gloomy threatening sky, same lonely sea. No sail in sight nor yesterday. Made it a rule to take the tiller for two hours and a half every evening.

" *Friday, 6th.*—Nothing in sight but a few wild ocean birds, called in Icelandic 'kria,' 'toendne,' 'malamukka,' and in Norwegian 'krukka,' which kept us company but did not light. Same weather.

"*Saturday, 7th.*—Marvellous the stillness of the sea. Dead calm. Made no way."

During the suspense, a supernatural gloom spread over not merely the ship, but the sea— right round the whole horizon, over the sky also, far and near ;

> " And we did speak, only to break
> The silence of the sea."

This is, moreover, the very sea where legends hint that gigantic reptiles, the monsters of past

ages, are still seen : of towering height, the giant
Octopus for one ; the fabulous Kraken ; rearing its
head and mane on high, the Sea Serpent also,
known to exist; in recent times, that possible
phenomenon, the Malström, with all its horrors
and seductive power. However the above may
be, a little bird one day, from some distant
country, perched on our bowsprit ; flew away,
returned again, and

> " As if it had been a *Christian* soul,
>   We hailed it in God's name."

Every night, owing to the phosphorus in the
sea, there played about the ship "in tracks of
shining white," flashes of brilliant splendour.   I
have found it impossible to withdraw my gaze
from this dazzling phenomenon, so intensely
beautiful was the effect, resembling gold and silver
plates, especially in the track of the vessel, spinning
round; and, at the same time, there have been
great streaks of light above, immediately overhead—the Aurora Borealis. I have seen this

only between nine o'clock P.M. and ten, not later, but in that short hour it appeared like a procession ; the different streaks would split, then draw nearer to each other ; separate once more, part wider, rally again, then *pass*, slowly—in perfect silence—right across the sky till out of sight. I have beheld this glorious pageant, but cannot explain the theory, or why it should all be so hushed—when the Powers of the air weave their colours and clash, as it were, into a million of startling varieties; without noise, when jarring to all appearance in disorderly confusion, or like ranks when told to countermarch, until, just like innumerable armies, they file off and pass away.

" *Sunday*, 8*th.*—Signs of snow in the sky. We thought some land was near, so many more seagulls.

" *Monday*, 9*th.*—I awoke by hearing shouts on deck. All hands were piped up in the middle of the night, so dark we dare not sail. Remembered the seagulls and lay to. Another gale dead against us from the east. Bitter cold. Days much shorter. Arctic winter coming on.

"*Tuesday*, 10*th*.—Gale became worse and worse, and drove us far to leeward. Waves mountains high. Took in all sail and lashed the tiller to leeward. Nothing more to do.

"*Wednesday*, 11*th*.—Dark and dismal. Same howling, whistling, fierce wind. Let out the floating anchor."

It was remarkable how well our craft behaved, and how bravely, without once giving over, she met the wild sea. The present gale was equal to the first, waves as high but, if anything, less violent, and we saved our gunwale from all further loss. But now,

> "The snow fell hissing in the brine,
> And the billows frothed like yeast,"

for the snow which had been threatening fell at last, and some of it remained upon the rigging.

"*Thursday*, 12*th*.—Eight days have we been

going without the sun, or a sight of any sail whatever but our own. Sky clouded since yesterday
week, but to-day the violence of the wind lifted the
curtain a few hours." It will easily be understood
we did not exactly know, at this time, in what
part of the high seas we were; we went by and entirely depended on dead reckoning, compass, log
and chart, unable to allow correctly for lee-way,
current, or the variation of the needle which in
the vicinity of Iceland is very great; and in the
present instance, were unable also to find our
latitude by quadrant, since there was no sun.
We knew the Faroe Islands were still to windward, but could only conjecture they were to
south-east, because in that part of the sky a certain
appearance of the clouds was similar to what I
had seen once before, when touching at those
islands, like a pile of plates, one cloud above the
other, each protruding, with a shadow in between.
Otherwise, we were entirely out of reckoning as to
the present course, whether it would be to north

of Faroe or to south; in which latter case it lay between Faroe and Shetland, so that I began to look out in south-east one evening for the light-house of Muckle Flugga, which stands upon a rock of the British Islands, at the extreme north end of Shetland. Two years previously to this, the present writer had been weather-bound one day upon the coast of Shetland, near the village of Ollaberry, and in the same house was a little boy, intended for the sea; a song, written out from memory for his special benefit, but only half remembered now, may properly come in here :—

> " Yet I have seen the angry waves,
>   Like giants in their might,
> O'erwhelm the best and bravest hearts,
>   And bear them from my sight.
> But, oh! I do not seek to change
>   The scene—whate'er it be—
> For never did I once regret
>   When first I went to sea.
>
> Oh! I have kept the midnight watch
>   Beneath a starry sky,
> And listened to the legends wild
>   That landsmen so decry :

For on the deep and **mystic sea**
There is **a sacred** spell,
Which none but sailors know **and fear,**
And none but them can tell.

I care not, they may scoff at us
Who safe in harbour sleep,
But ne'er can he forget his God,
Who dwells upon the deep!
A moment, and his dwelling-place
The sailor's grave may be,
But never did I once **regret**
When first I went to sea."

During the present heavy seas, on one occasion, when I was the only hand on deck and lying down in full waterproof, the sea washing clean overboard first covered, then lifted, and a few feet farther on deposited, the present writer; "a little farther," as the gunwale was somewhat lower than one's knee, and the only hand on deck might have "fared worse."

"*Friday*, 13*th.*—Gale evidently spent—fourth day. Lovely sky. Towards evening a favourable breeze, and first appearance of the moon.

"*Saturday*, 14*th.*—Gale from the west. Our

hopes are like the billows, rising high. Have
been going at full speed, nine knots. Saw a
stormy petrel; laughed at it.

"*Sunday*, 15*th*.—Began quite calm. Passed the
meridian at four P.M., and entered the German
Ocean, sailing satisfactorily." Night before last,
as we suppose, or between Friday and Saturday,
we passed the isles of Faroe, but they did not
come in view. On Sunday afternoon, in less than
two days later, the meridian of Greenwich; and
what is not generally known, at least not taught
in English schools, this, among northern nations,
is the boundary between the Atlantic and German
Oceans; all on the west of this line being the
Atlantic, all on the east the German Ocean, or
North Sea.

Our log now told us more or less where we
were, so as to enable us to estimate, not only the
exact distance the vessel had been driven back,
but in this way her very longitude; now east,
whereas it had hitherto been west. Our clock

upon the cabin wall was now put on three quarters of an hour, to be correct by where we were.

In taking the helm, our ship's compass being fixed under the cabin skylight that came so near the tiller as to be almost under one's nose, I was assisted, as most other pilots are, by the clouds : in the daytime keeping her up to the end of some cloud in the horizon ; in the night, which was easier, had only to keep her ahead for some star. And any star will do to go by, as all sailors know, when once decided on and followed for a time. This rude and simple map will give some faint idea by showing how the "hardy Norsemen" still divide and classify their stars. The way they have of calculating distances at sea, is by so many miles not in one hour, but in four hours, and, as their mile at sea is equivalent to four miles English, this way of reckoning will be found to correspond exactly with our own. But whoever would understand more fully the whole thing as practised by Norwegians, had better read up some guide to their technical terms, a lesson I was all the while most careful to avoid!

Once in the North Sea, we thought no more of " Muckle Flugga," having left it, by this time, far away to the south, but on Monday the 16th of September, " To our utter horror, the old enemy, Eastwind, returned with double violence and tore our mainsail. Saw another petrel; tried to laugh." Sailors are not much given to sentiment, but on making some remark that night to one of the men, upon the weeks we had been out and the days we might yet be, when both alone on deck, he answered me in his own Norwegian, " While we have food, there is hope. If our provisions fail, God only knows what we shall do. But while they last, here we can live, and hope for (*bedre Dage*) better days." I have translated these words almost exactly, from a note made at the time. And it must have been about this time that a pet sheep, which had come all the way from Iceland with us, and become the favourite of all on board, had to be slaughtered. The owner would not see it done.

During each of these contrary winds, when an Englishman would often have been tacking, my Norwegians did not appear to know anything about it; and this was no fault whatever in the ship, for to swamp it I would challenge any sea.

" *Tuesday,* 1*7th.*—Wind has gone down in the night, and a west wind is favouring us once more. Lovely day. Saw more than one rainbow, and a sail, the first one visible since fourteen days. *Except our own.*"

So then we bounded on; away she went, full speed, full sail, one tiny speck upon the great North Sea; and on the day after, having been now at the mercy of all winds, for three and twenty days the sport of their caprice, driven about the high seas in a most untraversable way, we saw land! The first appearance of that

welcome land, old Norway, consisted only of
tremendous cliffs, black, forbidding, and precipitous. It was along the whole horizon to the
east, and crested with *new* snow; which was worth
noticing, because we had set sail from Iceland
when the flowers were all in bloom; and whatever had been given me—by one whose gentle
hand will gather such no more—were long since
withered and dried up. And now the skipper,
for the life of him, could not say what part of the
whole coast this was; it had no leading outlines,
no one mountain that he could remember.

"*Wednesday*, 18*th*.—We have had, alternately,
dead calm, and heavy swell. Wind, present
moment, off shore. Land in sight all day, and
many sails. But this evening, some flashes of
lightning to windward; sky threatening; have
to keep outside." In the distance, a very large
steamboat, southward bound, was visible that
night with my binocular, coming, in all probability, from Archangel on the White Sea. But

owing to the darkness, we very nearly ran foul of another smack such as our own; she was crammed full of men, carried no lights, had simply a square-sail and was full built fore and aft in the old fashion, only to be seen now about the coasts and harbours of the very north, quite out of date elsewhere. Profiting by this escape we showed, as soon as possible, the proper lamps: red, for port or larboard side, green, for starboard—which wanted no end of looking to before they could be used, and took some time to light.

But now the land was no more visible; darkness came on, compelling us to lay to. At midnight however, now gently, then gradually increasing, arose a change of wind; it had been off shore, but this time was favouring us at last. The sky became clearer, coast distinct, we set every stitch of canvas and, thanks to the *lighthouses*, next morning entered Olafssund under all sail—having hit our port.

This was on Thursday the 19th of September,
after a distance of (how long, reckoning the devia-
tions, I dare not say, but direct) 800 miles.   Upon
this 800 miles, or so, I did not hear a word of
English, and scarcely did a syllable escape my
lips ; the skipper, three hands, and one man for
domestic purposes, being simple, very honest,
but uneducated Norsemen, who spoke only their
native tongue.   Such men will be always an
exception, but may prove the rule, or establish a
fact which appears to be universally the case,
would be acknowledged by all seafaring nations,
and is what I have found, that, if French is the
language of courts, English—is the language of
the sea.

CHAPTER IV.

NORWAY.

"Homeless, ragged, and tanned, under the changeful sky;
Who so free in the land, who so contented as I!"

The Vagabond.

IN the same year, '72, after some delay at
Aalesond (*alias* Olafssund, the port we
made), Trondhjem, Christianssund and
Bergen, nominally for the purpose of seeing
those towns, in reality more for the sake of being
cheered by human faces after so long an absence
from land, I struck out for the interior of this
peninsula of Scandinavia, intending to cross over
Norway on foot, from sea to sea; notwithstanding
the lateness of the season, which made that range
of mountains in the centre of the country very

hazardous to pass, because the autumn snow—
which falls at the commencement of arctic winter
about the middle of September—has had no
time to harden, and lies drifted over all the passes
on this backbone of the country very deep.
Aalesond, it may be as well to add here, is a
thriving sea-port and great rendezvous in summer
time for all the Spanish vessels engaged in trade
with Norway, but especially resorted to for
lobsters, of which whole cargoes leave here in the
season, ships laden for Spain with nothing else,
while the Norwegian children in the streets talk
Spanish as easily as any language of their own.
On landing here, the very first thing said and
commented upon within my hearing was a piece
of news by telegraph, to say the king of Norway,
Charles XV., was no more.   His Majesty had
only died the night before, and very suddenly.

Leaving these places and their trade, together
with all the usual observations on customs and
manners in Norway, the opening scene of this

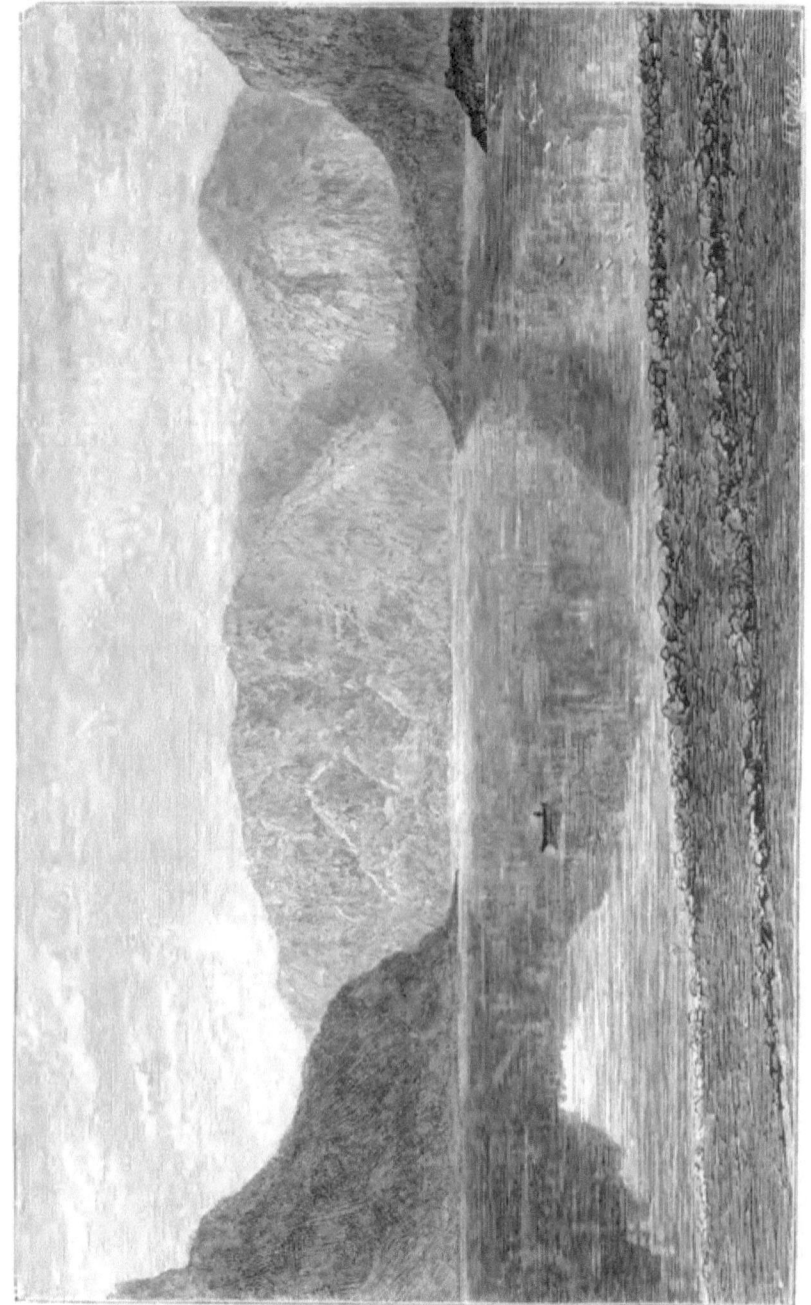

perilous expedition will be laid upon the Sogni
Fjord, where a little steamer had taken me from
Bergen, the only passenger on board. She went
up this narrow bay, or fjord, between tremendous precipices sheer down into the water on
each side, for between 70 and 80 miles to where
I landed—a station called Fronningen. From
that lonely and isolated country-house there lay
some distance yet, by water, to the village of
Urland, where this travelling on foot was to
commence; had it only been *later* in the season,
the intermediate part by water would have been
performed upon the ice, either in a sledge or by
skating all the way. As it happened, I had to wait
an hour and a half before it was possible to get a
boat or men to undertake it; but then began some
scenery of real magnificence, which lasted the
whole time I continued in this open boat—four
hours—during which time we made no less than
17 or 18 miles. The language spoken by these
boatmen was entirely a *patois*, difficult to under-

stand at first, and I found afterwards was different in each province or *Amt;* but the Norwegian language, alluded to before as spoken on board ship and in the towns, is the same as Danish *precisely*, both in pronunciation and in spelling, with only a slight difference of accent, as we find in every language not confined to any one city or kingdom.

Old and familiar scenery now greeted the adventurer, as I passed in measured time on calm, still water between mighty cliffs, and drew near to the village of Urland, which in order to behold without delay I left the boat and climbed a rising ground, just where the land projected, because it was no doubt that letters would be waiting there, or news at all events in some shape, of or from those who had been told to write to this address. Moreover, I had gone in here for salmon fishing, as two famous rivers come down from the mountains near this place, one extending four miles, the other (in a separate valley) for three miles or so. These rivers were

VIEW OF URLAND, SOGNI FJORD.

on lease for many years, and last season two rods
had taken in the river first mentioned 900 lbs.
of salmon and sea trout; this was in less than a
month, and would have amounted to a great
deal more in that time even, if the want of water
in the river had not been so very much against
it; none were landed over 20 lbs., but some were
of 19 lbs., and 60 lbs. was thought a good day's
sport. The season here commences rather late,
in fact not till the middle of July; begins, in
one sense, at the middle of April: but there is
no use in fishing this river so soon, partly by
reason of its distance from the open sea, partly
for the swelling of this and every river by all the
melted snow upon the mountains. The primitive inhabitants of this isolated and secluded
valley showed signs of welcome to the present
writer, who had come to live among them, as it
would appear, once more. Circumstances connected with his father and predecessor had given
him great hold upon the hearts of the people,

and as they gathered round the house that evening, Saturday, a ball was given to them in the open air.   Dancing went on till midnight; one of the villagers volunteered his fiddle, and came out with a great number of very old Norwegian airs—time honoured—which had no doubt inspired merriment upon the holidays and rejoicings of many generations before him.   A considerable number of both sexes had assembled by this time; the liquor of the country was served round, the moon rose, dances of every variety succeeded—some undoubtedly of great antiquity —a tar barrel was set on fire, burned for twenty minutes while the men stood in groups and sang in chorus many of their ancient songs, one with a tune like the "Hardy Norseman," another very lovely song, "Vort land! vort land! vort foster land," which recalled to me indefinable impressions of a previous state of existence—

Ere, sure as Hindoo legends tell, I left our parent climes afar,
Immured in mortal form to mourn—

so that I called for it again. After which
the blazing barrel was turned into the waters
of the fjord and floated, with the current
of the salmon river, right out into the middle
of this land-locked scene, only half extinguished,
the other part burning brightly above water
and reflected, far and wide, upon the cliffs
and precipices of the bay!

" *Monday, September 30th.*—Left Urland at
one o'clock, with Hans and Edelinck and horse,
for the mountains, but the winter appeared to
have set in. Reached Singeraim—arriving after
dark." The pack-horse was conveying sundry
luxuries for some future time, perhaps next
summer, to complete a shooting-box built upon
the mountains by my orders—baggage, such
as the canteen and bed valise I had become
accustomed to in Iceland. Hans and Edelinck
were two men from Urland, the village, who
did not exactly perceive what the object was of
going up into the mountains at this season of

the year. I had to remind them, as an en-
couragement, of what really had no colouring of
reason (and therefore with considerable em-
phasis), that now it was the *pairing season* of
reindeer throughout all Norway, commencing
to-morrow, October 1st. "Now or never! Let
us heed it! let us profit by it!" Accordingly
we trudged on till the road ended, where a
splendid lake inland, called Vasbygd, between
precipices wholly perpendicular, and rising like
towers from the very margin of the water, had to
be crossed by boat; and here again I was disappointed by not being able to cross upon the
ice, which was at least expected on this lake, of
which the waters are in summertime extremely
cold. In consequence of this I had to wait, with
all the baggage and one man, upon the far side,
until our horse had circumvented the water, by
going with the other man a long way round. After
this matters became more simple, and the ascent
began. Winding up a narrow glen by a rocky

pathway, sometimes half way up the very face of the cliff, with just room enough to tread, we followed the course of a foaming torrent for three hours, having the abyss upon our right, where this river was roaring below in one cascade after another, which from time to time burst in full view upon us, while we continued going up and up, with an overhanging cliff upon our left. Opposite, across the gorge, cliffs rose for thousands of feet, and formed different summits, which I can only compare to the heights and precipices of Abyssinia; from some views once shown to me, of what in fact bore a very great resemblance.

That night we came to anchor at a lonely habitation, placed like an eagle's nest upon the cliff, built of the stunted pine-tree wood that grew here and there upon the rocks in all manner of places, wherever the roots found any earth. It was a shepherd's cabin, the only human dwelling in all that region, and we gathered round the fireside of the family. Being miserably exhausted by to-day, from the want of previous exercise, I fell into a heavy slumber; and on waking accidentally next morning from a semi-torpid state, was greeted by the presence of long icicles outside the window which was at my feet.

" *Tuesday, October 1st.*—Piercing cold and dreary. Left at ten o'clock. Reached Aurdal somewhere about four." This latter place was a kind of village, even more remote, and situated very beautifully on a level where the gorge was wider and the river flowed without that deafening noise of which I had begun to feel very weary; for until now that river had been one succession of cascades, owing to the great height of these mountains, which were only accessible by the one pathway, very steep and winding, that we have been following two days; and have now arrived at the height of several thousand feet above the sea. Here we

shall have to send for the old deerstalker, who
lives a whole day's journey from this place (not
that I entertained any hope of killing reindeer
now), but because he was wanted as a guide
over the passes. So here we have to wait, as if
detained in prison, with nowhere to go, nothing
to do, and scarcely enough to eat, besides,
what was more painful still, no occupation
for the mind. But here as a consolation the
scenery was of surpassing magnificence; atmosphere so clear as to resemble that of the En-
gadine; pine forest on every side, stunted, but of
great extent; overhead, enclosing us, the loftiest
summits of this range completely covered with
snow; while the log cabins, which were to be
my abode, gave it an appearance of tranquillity
and home comfort, together with an appearance
of *life*, which this dread winter was unable to
dispel.

> " Life! I know not what thou art,
> But know that thou and I must part:

> Yet when, or how, or why we met,
> I own to me is a secret yet.
> Life! we have been long together,
> Through pleasant and through cloudy weather.
> 'Twere hard to part with friend so dear;
> Perhaps, 'twill cost a sigh, or tear.
> Then steal away! give little warning,
> Say not good-night, but in some happier clime
>   Bid me good-morning!"

Hans now entered into my project of walking from here over to Christiania; but Edelinck, the other man, I had to dismiss, also his horse with him.

" *Wednesday, 2nd.*—No appearance of Knudt (the old Huntsman). Climbed the rocks to see if he were coming. Am deeply gratified by the surrounding scenery, but find it empty. Am depending on these Norwegians, and have to wait their time, wasting the days away. But they have been a long time Norwegians, and it will be a long time before they be any other kind of people.

" *Thursday, 3rd.*—Saw the village inside as well as out. Examined sledges, tried snow-shoes,

practised the use of them. **Got into more than**
one bag made of reindeer skins, **which these**
people sleep **in when** upon **the chase. Heavy**
fall of snow.   I made a blazing fire!

" *Friday*, 4*th.—*Still a **prisoner. Remained**
faithful to the same log cabin, and made it comfortable.   Same haunch of reindeer meat.   Made
a fire of juniper, which crackled up at **once, and**
left a strange but very agreeable perfume.   This
evening, behold! Knudt came, **the old stager,**
and all the hamlet assembled round my fire to
meet him.   Heaped on more logs, **to make a**
blaze, and more, to take off the **attention of the**
people.   We were surrounded."

This trusty Yäger (or *huntsman*) had been in
the service **of my** family for many years.   When
his late master **was no** longer able to walk in
pursuit of the reindeer, during the **last** year **of**
that master's life, this old servant **would bring**
out the sledge; and when my father was **com-**
fortably **seated,** would guide **his horse over all**

the places where it was possible for a horse and
sledge to go, in the heart of the reindeer territory,
wherever any had been killed in former days.
And now, while the tones of his voice, which
were familiar, rang out by this fireside, they felt
like some well-remembered echo of the past—
like some commanding echo, sweet and clear,
from mountains eternally guarded by this everlasting ice and snow; on oases of which, so far
as he was able to remember, this grand old fellow
had commenced his life, and on which he was
prepared to end it. Our meeting here was joyous,
but moderated in expression, from his lifelong
familiarity with danger; while his words, the only
words he uttered for some time, "Velkommen
til Norge," were followed by a silence in which
no one spoke, and the tear was there upon his
cheek, as he continued, without moving where
we stood, to hold my hand.

"*Saturday*, 5*th*.—More snow. Stupendous
mountains bar the way—impossible to pass

them while it lasts. I am become the slave of a cowardly solicitude, lest, in the heart of this dread winter there lurk the seeds of disappointment to my vehement desire, of gaining the opposite sea. But I do not submit.

" *Sunday 6th.*—Turned out a lovely morning. Aided by the old man, I formed my company, and four able fellows, two natives of the place, Hans who came from Urland, with Knudt himself, who came from dear knows where, provided themselves with snow-shoes, one sound pair each, with one also for myself, to be used whenever we should gain the table-land above." This village or hamlet of Aurdal being close under the level of perpetual snow, its inhabitants understood by nature the use of these contrivances and how to make them; going over trackless snows, where they have practised it since childhood, as it were " like a streak of greased lightning!" The snow-shoe, or " snae ski," is eight or ten feet long, consisting of a simple plank of the Norwegian pine made narrow, fastened at the middle by twigs over the boot, pointed and turned up at one end right ahead, to prevent it catching anywhere; the same kind of thing is pretty generally used by every tribe or nation above a certain latitude right round the globe.

At this lonely cluster of habitations, the last day of our detention passed pleasantly enough; but towards evening, when the sun had set, a thick mist rose upon the place extending far and wide. I turned in early to be ready for next morning, feeling sure the day would come out bright and this fog pass away; but so thick was it now that not one single object could we see outside the door. Still it was the last night of my imprisonment. To-morrow I had determined, to escape, let Fortune do her worst, and all the elements combine to block the way. It happened the last moment before turning in, that I looked out of the window; and there, where nothing had been visible before, at somewhere

about twelve yards' distance, black with a kind
of transparent hue, there stood, or appeared, or
showed itself, a deep shadow.   Thinking it might
be a parting of the mist, I watched a long while,
but in vain—the shadow never spread.   I made
no remark to the old man, who was still in the
room, but before leaving me that night I told
him to look out of the window; and he saw,
in the same direction, the same thing.   What it
was, he said, with no slight agitation—speaking
under his breath—might be secretly explained,
by there having been buried underneath that
very spot, *in unconsecrated ground,* ever since
this gloomy solitude had become the scene of
human habitations, the bodies of their dead!

" *Monday, October 7th.*—The mist has gone
entirely, completely cleared away, and left no
traces.   But the clouds that have risen from the
gorges of these mountains form a close canopy
above, and hide the sun."   Five in number, we
crossed the last of those rude bridges that span

the winding torrent; frail, rickety, made of
timber, and the rocky pathway led us upward,
still higher, still wider remote from the habitations of mankind. At twelve o'clock however
we halted, at an isolated farmhouse, just a roof
and four walls, which had been deserted for the
winter, only used in summer by the shepherds,
who at the same time bring their wives and families
to this and many more such temporary houses,
calling this kind of house a "Saetter." Here
we all turned in, rested a bit, held a consul-
tation, and partook of the same refreshments;
but the cold was so freezing and intense we
found it impossible to wait. I lost no time
in getting into motion. Stembergdalen (the
name of this hovel) was the termination of the
actual ascent; from thence our way continued
onward over trackless wastes, interminable and
dreary, with nothing to be seen henceforward far
and wide but everlasting snow; save here and
there some gloomy lake, which was invariably

frozen over. Up to this time, as the path had been always more or less distinct, we had each kept some distance apart, in single file, myself in advance, the old man bringing up the rear; but now he was called forward, we all kept near together, and he pointed out the way. The snow was in good order for this first part, so he gradually fell behind, and I went on until summoned by a halt—it must have been some three hours afterward—when all collected by a rock which had no covering of snow, and Knudt the old huntsman, still hale and hearty, wonderfully upright for his age, pointed out to each one by what sloping valleys in the snow, frozen lakes, and isolated rocks, the unseen path now lay. But this very same Knudt, the man I chiefly depended on, had evidently seen his best days; and now humbly implored me to let him return, declaring it was utterly impossible for him to go on—in fact, there was no help for it. Unable to bear the least insinuation that his strength was no longer the same, this old fellow had set out with me, regardless of his own safety, and resolved if possible to follow; so that now, after some deliberation while I also gave him orders for the summer following, we parted, and on taking leave he kissed my hand.

We watched this old man of the mountains retire gradually in the distance, but soon saw he began to walk away unsteadily, as if tottering, and wholly past his work; therefore I very soon despatched one of the party who remained to help him, support his steps if necessary, and see him safely home.   ·

After this may be dated the commencement of our troubles; to lose two men, half my company, was a movement for which I was wholly un-prepared. Hans knew the way, having been up before on some business in one of the stone huts, where I had formerly stayed for deerstalking, but not in winter; and in the event of *crevasses*, the smaller our number the greater would naturally

be our danger. Landmarks at this season of the
year are covered up; what was worse, the snow
became softer as we went on, and very deep.
We sank in it up to our waists.

The only present remedy was in snow-shoes;
these were immediately strapped on, and while
the way continued over level snow we made
considerable head. But now daylight began to
fail, and the hut was known to be not less than
four hours' distant. Twilight came on, and the
appalling monotony of these dreary wastes, with
nothing but vast regions of snow visible on
every side, became evident upon the faces of
my men, which reflected the vacancy of this great
scene, while their eyes, like those of dead men,
wore a stare as if searching into empty space.

> " And here on snows, where *never human foot*
> Of common mortal trod, we nightly tread,
> And leave no traces. For the savage sea—
> The glassy ocean of the mountain ice—
> We skim its rugged breakers, which put on
> The aspect of a tumbling tempest's foam
> Frozen in a moment."

So, like those witches who speak thus in 'Manfred,' for ever onward, forward, where no creature that had life was ever able to continue or exist, we slided, we glided, far into the night. Frozen lakes appeared in front—appeared on either side —ghastly to look upon, frightful, horrible. And I felt as if gazing on that frozen region of the 'Inferno,' where the faces of the departed stare at one from their place of punishment or living burial in ice, to challenge whosoever may pass by.

Our rapid progress came however to a miserable end, when Hans, going over some pieces of rock he did not allow for in the darkness, contrived to snap one of his snow-shoes; making of course the other one comparatively useless and himself unable to keep up. I called a halt; and myself setting the example, gave the word to remove all snow-shoes from the feet, which was obeyed with an implicit, soldier-like obedience. Here we rested for a bit to eat and drink, while

darkness was increasing, but Hans declared there
was no doubt about the way. "Forward" again
presently, we rose and tried to get along, but
here was a wretched struggle. Floundering deep
in the snow sometimes we stuck, sometimes one
getting on ahead would disappear, while each
man struggled for his own life. Oaths and
curses in their language filled the icy air of
night; while the hoarse word of command was
given, shouting one by one, to keep together—
to be ready any moment with a hand, keep each
other in sight and not be separated by this
treacherous darkness, lest any one might sink into
a chasm. At every few yards we rallied, guided
by each other's voices, rested a little while and
then pushed on once more. In momentary ex-
pectation we should soon see something of the
hut, I frequently, whenever some rocks of any
size came near the way, rushed at one as it were
with open arms—only to recoil, withered and
blasted by the galling disappointment, like a

man who has been cheated of all he ever hoped, believed in, or lived for, to find it only a bare rock!

Time went on.   We have already been *twelve hours* on foot, and must have given up in blank despair ere this, only that Hans recognised his way and said the hut was somewhere close at hand.   What should be our joy, when too exhausted to give signs of it by shouts, but the sight of a bleached and wooden doorway, on the face of a black hill just above; here was our destination, here at length was to be the wandering spirit's rest!   On getting up to it, however, we found it frozen tight; but that was a trifling matter, and the present writer was let down into it through the skylight, by a rope tied round under his arms; landed on the table, and from that station arrived in safety on the floor.   The application of a good sized boot upon that door soon sent it flying open, and my men came in. We shook hands all round, lit a blazing fire—in

fact two fires, because there was a German stove
also—and as if it had been in the bosom of
Mount Hecla fed the flames, by chopping
timber with iron implements, axes and hatchets,
like anvils with resounding noise—while the
outside was covered with snow!

*   *   *   *   *

Tuesday, October 8th.—We found the hut *very
comfortable indeed.* This hut, by way of explanation, is only one of several that were built
by the writer's father and predecessor as boxes for
the season when stalking reindeer; they are from
fifteen to thirty miles apart, and command access
to the reindeer of this whole territory, for he
knew their chief places of resort who built these
huts to live in. Of this one, by name Baccahella,
the stone walls were four feet thick; had twelve
feet square of space inside, stones uncemented but
well lined with reindeer-moss, and I slept on a
bed of the same. To eke out a subsistence
whenever there might be no venison, as the sport

was extremely uncertain, here were on the shelf
whole tins of soup, and meat preserved, besides
lobsters hermetically sealed, and on the ground—
a dozen of champagne! These comforts (the
champagne was Montebello) are taken up on a
sledge beforehand, being sent out from England
in the spring, and conveyed here—likewise also a
supply of timber from the forest—when the snow
is hard.   Not to neglect the mind, here was also
some *pabulum mentis,* in the shape of a Danish
dictionary (very interesting, but sent me to sleep),
a ‘Life of Peter the Great,’ and the ‘Poems of
Ossian;’ which same poems of Ossian, even if
original, have no great signs of intellect, and
left me in a state of mind that one who reads a
long-continued record of wars, conflicts, murders,
killing one man here, another man there—unless
he is able to keep it up—must inevitably feel.
When Cairbar, who has already killed Cormac in
Temora “shrinks before Oscar’s sword! He
creeps in darkness behind a stone! He lifts the

spear in secret! He pierces **my** Oscar's side.
Their eyes roll **in fire.** **See gloomy** Cairbar
falls! The steel pierced his forehead, and divided
his red hair **behind.** **But never more shall Oscar**
rise. His spear **is** in his terrible hand! 'I hear
the noise of war.' A thousand swords are half
unsheathed. We first arrived. **We** fought.
We saw Oscar on his shield. **We saw** his blood
around, &c." Here are *two* **ancient worthies**
killed at once, falling by **mutual wounds.**

The canteen and **bed valise intended for use**
here which had **come** all the way from Iceland,
were sent away yesterday **with** Knudt **and his**
companion, my other men **each** having his own
burden, compelling **me** to make shift on the old
things of **last** year. But Lars, one of the two
who remained, undertook to slide away **upon his**
wooden instruments and bring such necessaries as
I wanted for a short stay here, promising **to** return
in two days. So as **the sun came out and the**
weather **became** really **fine,** I let him **go**; and

saw from the door, as he started, a whole flock of
ptarmigan get up, white as the whole scene, *in-
visible* before, and only to be marked when settled
by their shadow which the sun cast on the snow!
In the course of that afternoon I went out for
a walk with Hans, and saw a bridge within easy
distance of the hut, where it had been built the
previous summer by my orders to enable one to
cross a torrent in following the reindeer; found
it a simple wooden concern, all that was wanted,
but since then I hear it has been washed away.

Wednesday, October 9th.—Were shut in by a
howling winter hurricane, which swept the snow
high up all around about the hut, and threatened
to exterminate the light we had from that one
skylight on the roof. The hours went on.
While daylight lasted, Hans went about his
usual business, cleared away the dinner things,
chopped firewood, and spread the moss to make
my bed all tidy for the night; lit my candle on
the table somewhere about five o'clock, and then

sat him down by the log fire. Outside, all was
trackless, windswept, a waste of interminable
snow :

> " Where the traveller meets aghast
> Sheeted memories of the past ;
> Shrouded forms that start and sigh
> As they pass the wanderer by ;
> White-robed forms of friends long given
> In agony to earth—and heaven."

Hans became pensive. Our little stone fortress
afforded inside a silence that was literally *felt ;*
broken only by the parting of his lips, which
periodically sent out smoke from the well-worn
pipe for his tobacco. We were feeling sleepy
from its fumes, when what should be suddenly
heard—enough to startle any mortal man—but a
noise outside the door, like some one rapping !
and whoever, or whatever it was, the rap was
unmistakable (it was evidently meant). On
opening the door, shedding a flood of light over
the snow far and away, who should be our visitor
but Lars, true to his promise, as large as life, and
twice as natural, because there came with him

also another man, but on first entering both looked more like those sheeted figures of the past whom one would rather not detain, the falling snow having adhered to them all over, so as to make a white coat extra. The welcome, however, that I gave them was a real one, and if possible increased by their success, in bringing me some well-filled bottles of fresh milk, a thick blanket, and a couple of large salmon trout!

Thursday, October 10*th.*—Emerging from what might have been our tomb, we issued one by one to face the trackless regions of deep snow once more. This was between forty and fifty miles from any village or town. Leaving the hut early, already covered half way up, we did not care how violent the wind when danger such as burial within those walls now threatened our retreat. Each with his knapsack, and carrying at the same time his snow-shoes on one shoulder, for the first part of this pathless tract we plodded. Here the snow was not so deep, daylight more-

over made a **great difference, compensating for**
the fitful gusts **that, dead** against **our course,**
drove the **snow hard into our faces, freezing our**
very teeth. Presently we came **to a more level**
district, each man **quickly** slipped on his snow-
shoes and went ahead immediately for miles.   **So**
it went on after this alternately, now level travel-
ling, now getting over rocks, in which case we
had to drag our snow-shoes **with one** hand,
wielding with the other **hand** a walking-**stick, to**
steady one's descent from rock **to rock.   For it**
was evident **the** other side would **very soon be**
reached, since the snow **became gradually shallower**
as we continued **to get on;** descending by
degrees, **but with nothing more in sight to guide**
us than such mountains **in the** far horizon **as**
indicated **generally what** direction to pursue.
Yet here the **views** were strikingly **magnificent.**
Leaving behind **us the** two heights between which
Baccahella (the hut of **last night)** is situated,
Omsbraeen **and Vargebraeen, both** covered with

eternal snow, our course to-day lay downward
between Hallingskarven on one side, with Ule-
vasbotn on the other, both in the far horizon.
By degrees the scenery put on more of a grey
aspect, where the blackness of the rocks showed
under a thin covering of snow, and in time there
appeared before us in the distance a vast sheet
of water not frozen, as the lakes had been entirely until now. This was the lake of Strandafjord, which we made early that evening and
put up at a farmhouse—the place where Lars
had contrived to get his fish, milk, blanket, new
pair of snow-shoes for Hans, &c., &c.—for here
we have gained what may fairly be called *terra
firma.*

Friday, October 11*th.*—There being no occasion to wait here, I chartered an open boat and
followed the direction of this considerable piece
of water so far as it went, between splendid crags
crested over with new snow! On landing at the
other end I dismissed our third man, and went

ahead once more on foot right down a winding valley—still upon the snow—to Guldbrandsgaard, a thriving village, that appeared to be situated exactly where the snow left off, and came in there shortly after dark, once more among human habitations.

From here we had for the first time a road to walk on, to Christiania, all among deep forests in the very heart of Norway; making the whole distance, from the point of departure on the Sogni Fjord to the above named city, one of 185 miles. Whoever would understand the difficulties of this journey must consider not so much the distance but the time of year, inclemency of season, utter want of proper food, and kind of country, so thinly inhabited, by which I had to pass. Still we have now descended upon the interior of Norway, and henceforward I shall be, as hitherto, alone among the natives; so here I put on the costume, and came out in blue stockings, shoes with buckles, knee

breeches, fur waistcoat, and a jacket something
like that worn at Eton only blue, with silver
buttons on each side in front, while surmounting
the upper region was a cap, such as the peasants
wear, to keep the head warm and hang down,
whatever there might be to spare, upon one
side.

Speaking by this time the provincial also, I
became fairly domesticated in that house at
Guldbrandsgaard; nevertheless, on "*Saturday,
12th,* proceeded to Aal, along the banks of a
mighty river, through deep forest. Towards the
end in complete darkness, passing by timber none
so huge in Europe. On foot this day for eleven
hours." Once having got my men fairly out,
they went along. Strange to say, we saw no
wolves, nor any capercailzie, blackcock, hazel-
hen, or other fowl so thoroughly described in
various books on Norway. Our route was entirely upon the *king's high road,* as it was called,
where all the *carrioles* drive up and down in

summer-time with tourists, **for which** reason I
refrain from giving **the particulars of** stopping
at each place, or **describing any more of what**
the public will **not care to know.** It was **cold**
even for the **time of** year; notwithstanding **this,**
we had **to cross lake** after lake in open boats
which a month later might have **been** accomplished without the slightest obstacle by one
well-built sledge, and a pair **of tame reindeer,**
instead of having **now to** steer **our course**
between no end of floating timber **on its way**
to Christiania by the rapids.

It was **in ten** days after **setting out** from
where I put on the costume, **on Monday,**
October 21st, that **we** beheld **the** sea! the
Skager Rack, **that arm of** it called Christiania
Fjord. **Here** at last, with infinite delight, I
have arrived **over** trackless snows, past wilder-
nesses of dense forest, **between** tapering **pines,**
extending over so many **hundred** square miles
of country; but not till **after having** contem-

plated by moonlight **the deep** solitudes, silver
lakes between chaotic **mountains and** steep crags,
that constitute **the** bulwark **of this** northern
boundary **of the Old World.**   **At** times the
way has been monotonous, barren of incidents,
and dreary; but before closing such an imperfect account of this long journey, I wish **to**
endorse **a remark by** that great, **yet** comparatively
unknown traveller, **John Ledyard.   Two** years
previously to this, **the** present **writer** went **on**
foot from end **to end of** Shetland (the isles
of Shetland **being also part of** Scandinavia, not
of Scotland, geographically) **sailing** from one
island to another, **and** in that archipelago had
spent a considerable time; **their boats** are, by the
way, **built on the same plan as in** Iceland,
Norway, and the Faroe Islands—entirely different
to what **we find in Orkney or** anywhere upon the
coast of Scotland.   **But this man above men-**
tioned, after serving **under Captain Cook** in the
Pacific as a common hand, then undertaking

various expeditions to discover the north-west passage on his own account, for one of which Paul Jones prepared with him, finally saw his way to make the tour of the globe from London eastward on foot. Going up right round the Baltic he arrived at Petersburg, crossed the steppes of Russia, passed the Ural Mountains, entered Siberia, and in a year or so came within sight of the last stage—Kamtschatka. But here, he was arrested by order of the Empress Catherine of Russia—no one knows exactly for what reason —and brought back to St. Petersburg in chains.

He died not long afterwards at Cairo, in Egypt, thirty-seven years of age, intending to explore the unknown regions of Africa, and to establish communication over the interior by traversing this continent from sea to sea. And in his corre- spondence, what I shall endorse is where he says : " I have observed among all nations, that the women are the same kind, civil, obliging, humane, tender beings. They do not hesitate, like man, to perform a hospitable or generous action ; not haughty, nor arrogant, nor supercilious, but full of courtesy ; industrious, economical, ingenuous ; more liable in general to err than man, but in general also more virtuous, and performing more good actions than he. I never addressed myself in the language of decency and friendship to a woman, whether civilized or savage, without receiving a decent and friendly answer. With man it has often been otherwise. *In wandering over the barren plains of inhospitable Denmark, through honest Sweden, frozen Lapland, rude and churlish Finland, unprincipled Russia, and the wide-spread regions of the wandering Tartar, if hungry, dry, cold, wet, or sick, woman has ever been friendly to me, and uniformly so ; and to add to this virtue, so worthy of the appellation of benevolence, these actions have been performed in so free and so kind a manner, that if I was dry, I drank the sweet draught, and if hungry, ate the coarse morsel, with a double relish."*

To conclude, we entered Christiania by the West end or fashionable quarter of the town, and made for the *Hotel Scandinavie*, in the heart of the Norwegian capital; but I had some doubts on first beholding the edifice whether they would let one in, having only a peasant's costume, or direct me for a vagabond somewhere else.

I went that same evening to the theatre, but it was hung with black on account of the late king; the whole city, squares and terraces, appeared also, when daylight came, to be in mourning. So it was not *the season;* being, therefore, disappointed of festivity, I left Christiania with dislike, and returned as soon as possible to England.

CHAPTER V.

NORWAY.

"Huntsman! rest. Thy chase is done;
Think not of the rising sun.
For at dawning, to assail ye,
Here no bugle sounds *reveille*."

NORWAY, by a treaty which the late
Mr. Canning said once when not in
office, filled him with shame, regret and
indignation, became in 1814 the unwilling re-
compense to Sweden for the loss of Finland, of
which Russia, on the principle that might is
right, had taken possession. The Czar at that
time *guaranteed* Norway to Sweden, if the latter
would fall in with his project: and the reigning
sovereign of Sweden, Charles John XIV. (Berna-

dotte) was without difficulty persuaded to comply.
But since 1430 the Norwegian crown had been
united with that of Denmark, without any
interruption, and Norway been treated in every
respect as a province of the Danish monarchy,
until torn away by this treaty from its old
allegiance and given to Sweden; which had,
however, to concede to it a free constitution and
political independence, leaving little more than a
union of two separate crowns, in one dynasty.
Christian VIII. of Denmark—the same prince
who as viceroy of Norway refused to submit to
this treaty, endeavoured in the general struggle
to win the throne of Norway for himself, helping
in this way the kingdom to its independence.
The present form of government is such that if a
measure pass the parliament for three successive
years, the king refusing his consent to it each
time, that measure will become law without any
sanction from his majesty. This form of government—resembling a separate kingdom, under the

same crown—is similar in some respects to that of Hungary, of Iceland *now*, and of the Isle of Man. But the attempt to restore the same in Ireland is utterly chimerical and illusory, like a mirage. The whole movement is a rope of sand; its partisans have split among themselves; the other day I saw two "Home Rulers" of opposite opinions contending for the same seat in parliament. It would be simply to repeal the Union, and we might "as well talk of restoring the Heptarchy."

The project of Scandinavian unity has played no small part in days gone by, and needs but a slight opportunity to appear again before the public. It may be therefore of some interest to recall the principal features of its past history and to calculate its horoscope, for the future. At the close of the fourteenth century Queen Margaretha, called the "Semiramis of the north," a woman of great intellect, succeeded in combining the three crowns of Denmark, Sweden, and Norway.

Through many vicissitudes this union lasted until the beginning of the sixteenth century, when the too hard rule of Christian II. drove the Swedes into rebellion—when Gustavus Vasa, taking the command, founded that dynasty which afterwards gave Sweden kings like Gustavus Adolphus and Charles XII. Since that rebellion until now Sweden has been a separate kingdom from Denmark, and as for the respective sovereigns, their disposition towards the project of unity has been entirely dependent on their chances of gaining or losing by it. " Swedish kings and heirs to the throne at different periods have flattered themselves with hopes of being chosen successors to childless Danish monarchs; at such times every endeavour to kindle the flame of national sympathy and to prompt the wish for closer unity between the peoples enjoyed the most gracious protection from above. But if no such chance presented itself royalty and statesmanship were inclined to turn the cold shoulder upon

popular aspirations, and to regard as idle idealists
and ambitious demagogues whosoever ventured
to claim any community between the nations."
Sad as the above may be, we have a noble
instance of unselfishness and far-sighted diplo-
macy on the part of Sweden's present king,
Oscar II. grandson of Maréchal Bernadotte
(Charles XIV.), who has openly expressed his
wishes of making Scandinavia one empire, by
waiving his own rights to the throne of it. May
we not therefore hope the successor of Christian
IX. will at some future period, as the representative of that royal family so closely connected
with our own, unite in his person the whole
sovereignty of Sweden, Denmark, Iceland, &c.,
and Norway? making an empire worthy to
compare with Russia, if only in extent.

The more the German nationality becomes
consolidated, the more will a necessity be acknowledged by surrounding nations of strength-
ening themselves in the same way, and of

obtaining the power to resist all further aggression by mutual succour, as well as by the unity of all their several departments and adjoining states. Italy and its adjacent islands have become one kingdom; hitherto the project of Iberian unity, by blending Portugal with Spain, has been rendered impossible; but that Scandinavianism is tending this way there can be no doubt, and though it has twice broken down just at the point of trial, it is sure to gain at last sufficient strength for holding the three nations together, and making them join hand in hand for action at the hour of need.

It has been mentioned in a previous page, that all the kings of Norway and Sweden since these two became united have been crowned, with only one exception, at Trondhjem; accordingly we are now to witness the coronation of His present Majesty, Oscar Frederic, Duke of Ostrogothia: also of Her Majesty, Sophie-Wilhelmine-Marianne-Henriette, his Queen, daughter of

William the late **duke of Nassau.** It may be as
well **to add** here **the reason for which** the late
king's daughter and apparent heir, Louise-Jose-
phine-Eugénie, Crown Princess **of** Denmark,
did **not** succeed to him : namely, on account of
the Salic Law, which prevails in Sweden.

It **was** on a July evening, 1873, that I saw
from the hills above Trondhjem, **where I** lay **at**
ease, occasionally throwing down **a** stone, our
five ships of war enter **the** harbour—*Agincourt,
Northumberland, Hercules, Sultan,* and *Valorous*
—to escort **H.R.H.** Prince Arthur, on board
the Admiralty **yacht,** *Enchantress.* The king
arrived on the same day from a visit to the
North Cape, having met the queen upon the
way, who came here **very** wisely by Romsdal, a
route where the scenery of Norway is of surpassing grandeur ; and Her Majesty had been received
on board ship **outside** of Trondhjem by the
king, who there **at once,** on deck, affectionately
saluted her. His Majesty described afterwards,

in conversation with the writer, the ascent of
this North Cape, where one has to climb up from
the sea-shore, as being similar to his experience of
the Great Pyramid in Egypt, where three men,
exactly in the same way, are necessary to help up
the traveller. It is upon this cape, at the time of
the summer solstice, that the sun appears above
the horizon " for several days together without
setting," and then travellers are favoured with
what is called "a view of the sun at midnight."
One felt inclined to answer, "so may that Sun,"
which sets neither summer nor winter upon the
British Empire, " now shine upon your Majesty
at all seasons, and make your reign as prosperous,
as all assembled in this place desire."

Eight days the festivity went on without a
break, or anything to mar the public happiness;
" nothing was seen or heard but sounds of pleasure and festivity." Every evening the Hotel
Britannia held a *table d'hôte* for ambassadors,
naval officers, members of the diplomatic body,

and all present officially on this occasion; the
same wine I had tasted the year before at
Reikjavik, Chateau d'Yquem, at the house of old
Siemsen, the Norwegian consul in Iceland, poured
out and set before us by his lovely daughter
Rosa, was very much in fashion here, and flowed
"like a free and sparkling river."

Two days after the representatives of all
nations had assembled, the coronation took
place. That ancient cathedral was once more
thrown open which has been so celebrated in
the past, and in that part of it they have been
able to preserve I saw the grand old ceremony,
which it would be impossible, without the deepest
veneration, to behold. It is strange that in
a country like Norway, notwithstanding its traditions, the native aristocracy should have been
extinguished, and be no longer recognized by
the government at Christiania; moreover people
say at their suppression by the Norwegian parliament, the debate took the following rude form :

CATHEDRAL OF TRONDHJEM, INTERIOR.

To face page 191.

Count ——— said, "If that order is abolished to which I belong, I bid this land, my native hills and rocks, *farvel;*" then some one rose upon the other side, "and your native rocks will *echo* in reply, *vel*" (very glad to hear it).

So I sat next to the Brazilian ambassador, and we compared opinions in French; I would rather have been able to roam over the edifice, watching the ceremony from behind some pillar. Opposite, however, were the ladies, every one dressed in white, by Her Majesty's particular desire. We waited patiently, and in due time the coronation anthem rose, at first softly, soon gloriously —"wakening thoughts that long have slept." Presently these arches rang with music from the animated, well-timed, enthusiastic assembly of voices round the organ, when His Majesty the king, taller than any one beside him, came in view; and the whole procession wound in slow and measured pace, right down the central aisle.

First came all those who wore the Order of

the Seraphim, then came the Queen, attended by
her maids of honour, then came His Majesty
the King—followed by a glittering concourse.
Two thrones had been prepared opposite each
other very near the chancel, or rather on each
side a throne at this end of the nave, and
presently on these, while music still continued,
their majesties had taken seat. The service then
began, and after it had proceeded for some time
the king went up to the altar, then sat facing it
upon some cathedral chair while the Bishop
of Trondhjem anointed his forehead with oil,
making the sign of the cross, and afterwards
his chest, when the Bishop passed his hand underneath the royal shirt, the oil being contained in a
little golden horn said to be as old as any relic in
the whole of Norway. Some delay arose in
changing the robes His Majesty had on, which
were ducal, and had now to be exchanged for royal,
by reason of the chains and orders that were sus-
pended round his neck; this was done by dign

TRONDHJEMS DOMKIRKE, SØNDRE SIDEGANG I HØICHORET.

To face page 193.

taries of the Church of Norway (Lutheran) in vestments.

Once more the Bishop came forward, this time bearing in his hands the crown, which, by the assistance of those other ecclesiastics, now became placed on the king's head, and was immediately announced by a herald in loud voice to the assembled multitude, followed by cannon from all the men-of-war in the harbour acting upon some signal from the cathedral tower, and well-sustained, for every ship had twenty-one to fire, English, Prussian, French, Swedish, Danish, and Norwegian. When this had subsided, while a very beautiful hymn was being chanted by the orchestra above, and the king had returned to his throne, the queen came before the altar as His Majesty had done and took her seat, entering with a womanly appreciation into the whole scene. But when the crown was placed upon her head and adjusted by her maids of honour she was led before the king upon

his throne; and there, before all in that stately
edifice assembled, made him, with her crown
on, a bow that I shall never, while this life
continue, be able to forget. One felt as if
"ten thousand swords must leap from their
scabbards to avenge even a *look* that might
threaten her with insult."

The royal palace of Trondhjem, occupied
by their majesties for this occasion, was built
entirely of wood, and is the largest of that kind
in the whole of Europe; it was here on the day
following, that I, with two more Englishmen,
met our ambassador, and was presented. The
levée was held in a drawing-room of the palace,
its walls painted with various figures and designs
on wood: it had a ceiling of great height,
which gave the room an appearance of enormous
size. All bowed low, on either side the whole
length of the room, from end to end directly their
majesties came in; the spangled habiliments,
various decorations and abundant orders which

foreigners invariably wear, making the diplomatic
corps on every side give this levée a brilliancy
hardly anywhere to be surpassed; and the king
first, then the queen although no ladies were
presented, came round to where every man stood,
speaking the different languages with perfect ease,
the king himself shaking hands with us and very
graciously, so that we did not kiss the hand as
I expected.

Two balls were given, one by the city of
Trondhjem to the royal family and all visitors
on this occasion, making an assembly of twelve
hundred people; the other given at this very
palace by the king and queen, to not so large
a company, but hundreds of the peasantry from
far and wide, who perseveringly remained by
night and day in front outside, *made up the
difference.* At the first of these two balls, I
noticed, with regard to Norwegian etiquette, that
all came in full uniform, the ladies in ordinary
ball-dress; at the second, I saw on the contrary

that every lady came in white, by Her Majesty's
desire. Dancing went on with scarcely any in-
termission the whole time; we all joined in
heartily to the sound of delicious music, or
roamed over the palace from chamber to
chamber, "by wayward fancy led," wherever
paintings or refreshments made it desirable
to go.

Previous to this palace ball, there was on the
same day a naval review; his majesty visited one
ship of each nation, but of the English squadron
two. Lunching on board the *Hercules* I saw
every salute that was fired whenever the king in
his own boat approached the ships of either
nation; we saluted while he was making for the
Sultan, from which he visited the flagship—
Agincourt. From the ball-room at the palace
on that night direct, with a boatful of navy
fellows, I went on board the same ship and took
leave of Trondhjem: she weighed anchor at
1 A.M., and by the civility of Admiral Hornby,

since made a lord of the Admiralty, I went with
her to Bergen, a voyage of two or three days.
We had fair weather outside the whole time, and
I went on shore at last with great regret, having
fallen in to some extent with the routine, so
admirable and perfect on board a man-of-war.

But before closing this account, I take the
very greatest pleasure in bearing testimony to the
genial courtesy of His Royal Highness Prince
Arthur, since that time created Duke of Connaught : to that consideration for the feelings of
others, which as representative of our Queen on
this occasion, he so generously showed ; and to the
popularity among all classes and representatives
of foreign nations there assembled, which he won.

The evening which saw the departure of the
Agincourt, Northumberland, Sultan, Hercules
and *Valorous* for England, I spent outside of
Bergen at a country house, the seat of Herman
Janson, Esq., with an ancient avenue (for Norway)
leading up in front, and portraits of his ancestors

inside. As I sat upon the terrace with his family and watched the British squadron quit the harbour, that early history of Norway came home distinctly to my memory, in which we learn how Vikings, Norsemen, Danes and other nations of that race, by victories at sea gave kings to neighbouring lands. Here, in this very Norway, was the *cradle* of that Norman chivalry, which came over with the Norsemen who made Normandy, then spread south, east and west—by west I mean it spread to Ireland, as the conquest of that island under Henry II. was but a further wave of Norman conquest, after England had been vanquished in like manner by the same—and however we may neglect the customs of that age, or compare them with the adventures of Don Quixote, still

> " Hurrah for the Norman !
> The darling of story,
> His glory was pleasure,
> His pleasure—was glory !"

Retiring from the seaside to the mountains

which rise high in the interior of this great land,
to where in places the unbroken surface of snowy
plain and boundless deserts of eternal whiteness
shine calm and clear for ever, to a *hut* near
where the regions of pure snow assert everlasting
dominion, where huge rocks and majestic waterfalls inspire a man at once with awe, and his
whole life with solemnity: I went up by the
usual way, Urland, Larstondal and so on, a
distance of fifty miles from any village or town,
half gradual, half steep ascent, two days from
Urland, where the sea comes in; and anchored
on the last day of July—to leave out the particulars of stopping at each place—in a stone
residence or *hut* of ample size. Oh! the delight
of awaking on that morning after, in a region
where time has assumed larger proportions and
eternity appears to have commenced! I have
lived here in anchoritic seclusion, and been
absent from the world for months: and if the
life of contemplation treated of by Aristotle is

able to be realised on earth, *I* have realised it in that way. I have found it and enjoyed it alone among those mountains, like a heavenly calm, which none but those who have experienced it, can understand. But it is impossible, without some kind of being made expressly for the purpose to enjoy the tranquillity of that unbroken solitude, for the soul seems to escape from its prison-house when upon those heights, and I re-enter from that hermitage upon the customs and usages of civilized life—possessing the secret of a happy dream. I seem to have seen glimpses of some mighty mystery, heard whispers of eternal truth, and been tuned by the grandeur, by the profound magnificence of that wild and powerful scene—for the reception of a lofty wisdom. It is not the act of climbing a mountain, to behold a magnificent prospect and return that same night to your hotel; but to live, continue, *dwell* upon that boundless expanse, which does it.

I know no greater pleasure or delight, than to tread over regions of hard snow, when crisp and of a dazzling whiteness; it is like what the fish must feel when given back to its watery element, or the liberated bird, when once more able to soar high, cleaving far and wide the regions of pure air. To each of these, there is an escape from prison: and that is the feeling I have (though never yet incarcerated) while traversing the wastes of white, eternal, widespread, radiant snow. And when the sun, as in the Alps, tinges the summits at his rising with an edge of crimson, my spirit glows in response: having lived in the midst of these regions, and watched, in solitude, their glorious phenomena.

Truly, indeed, it has been said, "He that dwelleth mainly by himself heedeth most of others: but they that live in crowds, think chiefly of themselves. There is, indeed, a selfish seeming where the *anchoret* liveth alone, but probe his thoughts—they travel far, dreaming for ever of

the world.   And there is an apparent generosity,
when a man mixeth freely with his fellows; but
prove his mind, by day and night, his thoughts
are all of self: the world, inciting him to
pleasures, or relentlessly provoking him to toil, is
full of anxious rivals, each with a difference of
interest; so must he plan and practise for himself
even as his own best friend, and the gay soul of
dissipation never had a thought unselfish.   The
hermit standeth out of strife, abiding in a con-
templative calmness: what shall he contemplate,
—himself? a meagre theme for musing; he hath
cast off follies and kept aloof from cares; a man
of simple wants; God and the soul, these are his
excuse, a just excuse, for solitude.   But he carried
with him to his cell the half dead feelings of
humanity: there were they rested and refreshed,
and he yearned once more on men."

We pass on, however, to describe the *hut*
—one of a whole set which, scattered over
these mountains, give shelter to the deer stalker

by night when following the sport, very likely on
one day till sunset, and at sunrise the following
morning. This hut in particular, or shooting-
box, is at the elevation of 6,000 feet or so, and
commands a view in front of that enormous
glacier the Hardanger Yokul, of which there
are several summits, and the one called Kong-
snuten is exactly opposite my door, visible the
other side of a deep valley and loud-sounding
torrent, of great width in some places, which
rises in a large lake of extreme beauty within
easy distance of my habitation, embedded between lofty mountains crested on the summit
very often with new snow. The only vegetation far and wide, over huge rocks or even
on dry ground, is *reindeer moss:* and of this
I have come across a great many different
varieties, sparkling sometimes with frozen dew,
like new varieties again, which crystallises them
all over in the early morning. It is very
deceptive: like the crystal hunters, I have

been misled. To use the words of their own
song—

> "Sometimes, when o'er the Alpine rose
>   The golden sunset leaves its ray—
> So like a gem the floweret glows—
>   We thither bend our headlong way:
> And, though we find no treasure there,
>   We *bless* the rose, that shines so fair."

Inside my dwelling a large map of Iceland covers
one part of the wall; in fact, directly opposite
my door, so as to face the glacier out in front
whenever that is visible. But this tenement I
built is very similar to one described before,
Baccahella, only on a larger scale; the chief
difference being a separate compartment for
gillies, while the whole is more adapted for a
longer stay, so as to live without difficulty in this
peaceful, soothing region. And upon the lake
near by was kept a boat, as a part of the establish-
ment, called after one of the old Scandinavian
divinities whose name, by my Norwegians, is
still held in reverence—Baldur.

In the margin of a private journal, I find the following entry : "Washing, carpentering, shoe-making or boot-mending, cooking, and keeping all in order, the speciality of my man Hans :" a little later on, "Rivalry with difference of opinion between Lars and Hans, so that each man keeps doing his utmost to give satisfaction by his services, and cut out his opponent," which was only as it should be, and indeed a blessing in its way, as each did his best, so taking all the trouble of indoor affairs entirely off my hands. Lars, the first mentioned, was a regular deer-stalker, born and bred upon the mountains ; but the weather had been so unfavourable, alternately thick mist and heavy rain, that his talents had not once come into play.

One day we were thirteen hours walking, but saw no reindeer ; another day were caught in a snowstorm, which lasted five hours ; another day we crossed the glacier opposite, and came out upon a rocky desert, following by some *spoor*

but saw no reindeer, and slept out that night,
having been fully twenty-eight miles; another
day we went all round by Omsbraeen, Fagra-
nuten, Sandalshogda and Saata Yella (different
summits), for a walk of fourteen hours, without
seeing so much as a reindeer horn. On Sunday,
there would often be a general rendezvous
of shepherds, who lived in the neighbouring valleys below, and came bringing presents
of goat's milk, also of sweet berries, especially
Moltebaer, that grew wild where they lived,
hoping to reconcile me to the intrusion. They
first came to look me up on seeing smoke from
my hut in the distance, and on that occasion
brought some venison, thinking that perhaps I
had not been long enough upon the mountains
to get a shot, and hoping to win favour and protection by taking no money for it in exchange.
On ordinary days, if the weather made it hope-
less to go out, we moulded more bullets; and
if it cleared up towards evening had some rifle

practice at different ranges, so as to keep one's hand in.

I left this unproductive territory for a higher region two days farther on toward the east, where a hut has been built upon a rocky island, out in the middle of a splendid lake, and trusted to find the reindeer had retired in this direction where no shepherds ever penetrate, amid scenery of the wildest that can possibly be imagined. In getting there we had hard work to pass that lofty ridge or range dividing Hallingdal from Hardanger—snow in our faces and violent gusts of wind. Wishing, however, to have somewhat to show people after so long an absence, the elements made no impression while any chance of a reindeer still remained. Once it happened that a first-rate shot, my compatriot and fellow-countryman, Lord Antrim, who gave me the pleasure of his company in this part of the world one season, killed a reindeer the very first day of going out; but so scarce in these mountains have they since become, that hitherto I had not been so lucky as to get a single shot.

The circumstances connected with changing our retreat will be told best in words written at the time :—

"*Sunday, September 7th.*—Had to march. But first to cross the Strandafjord in open boat. Saw presently an actual live bear (*Björnsaerv*), but out of shot. Caught in a thick mist afterwards while plodding in deep snow. Found the lake (*Olia Vatn*), by using compass, and our hut, by boat.

"*Monday, 8th.*—Took boat, and landed in sight of two magnificent deer, without getting a shot. Followed them round by Galdehoiden and came home by Jungstarn. Saw, coming home by the lake, a ger falcon, pure white, at roost upon a mound.

"*Tuesday, 9th.*—Hurricane upon the lake has moistened our floor for us, this rock in the middle of Olia Vatn evidently 'porous.'

Thought of baling out the water. Had to stay
in all day for our lives. Bitter cold, as if it
were Siberia.

" *Wednesday*, 10*th*.—Fine morning. Took
boat; put Hans on shore for Urland as post-
man, I and Lars went on to look for reindeer.
Came upon one or two primitive stone shelters
for the night—work of ancient reindeer-hunters.
And a warren of white foxes' holes.

" *Thursday*, 11*th*.—Woke to see a reindeer
from my door, across the lake. But that mist
and snow combined which had driven us back
yesterday, while on the track in full pursuit,
continued to-day for a while—in fact, snow has
fallen daily during our stay here. Huntsman
and sole companion, Lars Lain.

" *Friday*, 12*th*.—Lake calm. Boat frozen, and
water-tight for once. Left the hut in good
order, but were obliged to leave for want of
fuel. Made our way with danger in the mist
over miles of boulders, slippery with snow and

holes between. Used the compass like at sea. Came upon a very ancient stonework over torrent, the work of reindeer-hunters. In time we escaped from the mist, then saw flocks of ptarmigan and wild duck."

Some people if they get a shot are so completely overcome, that when they fire it is a hundred to one whether the bullet goes anywhere near; a sort of trembling movement takes place, very disheartening to behold.* We had not been long out of the mist, before my huntsman and sole companion put his finger on his mouth, and began to hold me with a tenacity more easy to feel than to describe. I guessed at once

---

* Called the " Buck Fever." Symptoms of this are more than usually evident in some cases, extending over the whole human frame, but in general confined to the left arm, a member which may be detected oscillating gently, the patient's left hand being the part affected.

Cases have been known where this identical infirmity, by *scattering* the shot, has brought down actually *more* birds than would otherwise have come within the influence. But we are digressing.

what was in the wind, and began to feel sure by a kind of satisfied expression on his face that we had not been seen. Slowly and cautiously we trod, until from behind a friendly parapet of moss-grown rock, we saw a whole herd of reindeer exactly to windward at some distance, walking leisurely over a snow slope, right in the direction that we wanted. Speaking with but little breath, and remaining perfectly still as if suddenly changed into stone, Lars indicated how we should get at them, while both waited till they had passed over and were out of sight. In an instant we then started up, each with his rifle slung behind, so as to be free with both hands, and, like men who have been trained in a *circus* how to use their limbs, we clambered, we scrambled, we sprang from rock to rock, engrossed with one absorbing and passionate desire, which carried us lightly over the loose stones with ease. After some considerable distance in this manner, every sense on the alert, we halted, as Lars, pointing in strict silence broken only by low whispers, said we should have a peep over this next precipice. There they were! only two hundred yards off, and immediately below the precipice. We took our time, not to get into a "cast-iron sweat" about it, and singled out each one his reindeer—they must have been a herd of twelve or more, and I selected the buck. No sooner had I fired, than Lars began literally to blaze away; the herd, in a great state of alarm, hearing the broadside, but not knowing whence it came, hurried to and fro, lost the benefit of my second barrel, and at last made off right across the glen where we could follow them, as luck would have it, by the print of their hoofs upon the snow. Then Lars confessed he had been firing at the whole herd generally, and had succeeded (as it afterwards turned out) in grazing the antler of my buck. We got down and walked with considerable velocity, encouraged by signs on

the part of the animal I had selected (the head
buck of the herd) to lag behind. We lost
sight of him very soon, however, and did nothing
but follow on for something like two hours,
when, over upon the far side of a ridge, forsaken
by the herd, alone in the middle of a rocky
glen, there stood the noble animal! his head
turned away from us, and hanging down; his
whole frame showing signs of weakness (we had
seen blood on the snow while in pursuit), while
he remained motionless before us now as if in
a glass case. We approached within 150 yards.
I discharged both barrels without much interval
this time, and the animal gave a short bound
in the air, then disappeared behind a piece
of rock. It was evident he had fallen; so
eagerly did Lars my huntsman scramble over
rocks and boulders to the place, where now we
found him. There he lay, lifeless at my feet
upon the snow, his heart's blood spilt and glaring
out upon the frozen element beside him; both

bullets had entered the region of his heart, one had pierced also his lungs, that one fired at the very outset having wounded him in the neck. And the scarlet freshness of that blood upon the snow then made my senses tingle, and eyesight tremble; not because it was blood, vermilion like a red geranium, but as being so vivid a contrast—scarcely dispelled when I took up and began to handle a lump of crimson-saturated snow. His branching horns showed him to be ten years of age; which horns with head complete were quickly cut off by my hunts-man, who then flayed and quartered the animal, and buried the venison, whatever he was unable to take away, with large stones. Carrying as much as possible upon our shoulders, we presently came down to the lake side, crossed over in true character, correct Landseer colouring, and in the height of fashion (of the day). The head and horns were carried overland for eighty miles, from here down to the nearest corner of Hardanger Fjord, sometimes on horseback, sometimes on my back, in order to have something to show people after so long an absence, and ornament the inside of a London house in Portman Square.

How I love to hear the intellectual conversation of some sportsmen, and to watch men turning out for sport as the one sole and only business of this life, all in correct horse, dog, and gaiter style! showing that selfishness and very natural contempt for other people's interests, who may not care so much for sport, or may prevent it if coming in their way!

We slept that night in a Saetter or farmhouse among the mountains: from which I sent off Lars the next day early, to get everything ready beforehand for immediate departure, now that winter had commenced, and came on myself the day after with another man, who owned a horse, but had never been before this on the mountains—in fact I had to show the way for nine hours, guiding him over a pass. And I cannot say much for the horses in Norway, compared to those of Iceland, having tried more than one upon the mountains and found them comparatively unable to get on.

Striking out after this for a new region, in order to come down upon the Hardanger Fjord, I left the shooting-box described already with a horse and three men, snow being heavy on the house top and so far as the eye could perceive on every side. It was Arctic winter, and a glorious landscape for miles and miles in every direction. But that night was spent, after a whole day's forced march over the frozen regions, in a deserted Saetter where we did not arrive till very late, indeed, not until darkness had set in, when we did not know exactly where to find this abandoned, lonely habitation, and at last only found it after struggling for some distance in a marsh; then had to continue next day over quaking fens and Irish bog for fourteen miles, our horse very often wallowing deep in the mire ; which made it a very tedious business until we came to a respectable farm called Maurset, where we rested for an hour.

I pushed on from here to another farmhouse, close by the gigantic waterfall of Voringfoss, and slept that night within sound of its roar. On the day after, as we beheld this wonder of nature with its clouds of thick white spray, standing very near its base, our voices were scarcely to be heard for the deafening uproar which it made, while we shivered for the icy sensation produced by a cold and gusty draught, by currents of air from the falling of this water; and the very ground appeared to shake under our feet, while I continued gazing with a sense of awe and humiliation upon this lion of Norway, 900 feet high, allowed to be the highest waterfall in Europe. Deeply situated in a dark ravine, between precipices so perpendicular that no vegetation can grow upon their face, this monster, pouring and

roaring at this moment and for ever, has worn
away for itself a deep fissure between two precipices of great height, and will wear it deeper
still. While such is the peculiar beauty of
this waterfall in winter-time, when snows have
gathered thick around, and huge icicles in large
numbers, like stalactites, fringe every terrace
upon that gloomy chasm's walls, that scarcely
will any phenomenon be found in nature more
magnificent, extraordinary, or superb.

We arrived at the corner of that winding
narrow bay, Hardanger Fjord, and took the *Fjord*
steamer to Bergen, from which I returned to
England by the usual way, remaining late on deck
to contemplate the cliffs of this beloved country till
they were out of sight. And whether it may be
the writer's destiny to travel next in Egypt or
Abyssinia, Palestine, Arabia or Persia, Tartary
or Circassia, he will often remember and with
deep affection the time spent early in these
countries of the North—however badly, for want

of previous experience, the opportunities have been employed. And he would recommend to all who have the time to spare—begin with Scandinavia.

THE END.

LONDON : PRINTED BY WILLIAM CLOWES AND SONS, STAMFORD STREET AND CHARING CROSS.